John McGilchrist

Richard Cobden - the Apostle of Free Trade

His Political Career and Public Services

John McGilchrist

Richard Cobden - the Apostle of Free Trade
His Political Career and Public Services

ISBN/EAN: 9783744715447

Printed in Europe, USA, Canada, Australia, Japan

Cover: Foto ©Raphael Reischuk / pixelio.de

More available books at **www.hansebooks.com**

Yours sincerely
Rich Cobden

RICHARD COBDEN,

THE APOSTLE OF FREE TRADE.

HIS POLITICAL CAREER AND PUBLIC SERVICES.

A BIOGRAPHY.

By JOHN McGILCHRI

AUTHOR OF "THE LIFE OF LORD DUNDONALD," "MEN WHO HAVE MADE THEMSELVES," ETC.

BIRTHPLACE OF RICHARD COBDEN.

NEW YORK:

HARPER & BROTHERS, PUBLISHERS,

FRANKLIN SQUARE.

1865.

TO THE PEOPLE

OF

ENGLAND, FRANCE, AMERICA,

AND

THE INDUSTRIAL WORLD AT LARGE,

THIS HUMBLE ATTEMPT TO DELINEATE THE

CHARACTER AND CAREER

OF

"THE INTERNATIONAL MAN"

OF THE AGE,

Is Respectfully Dedicated by

THE AUTHOR.

PREFACE.

The leading purpose which the Author proposed to himself in his plan of this work, and which he has faithfully carried out in its execution, was to tell the story of Mr. Cobden's life and patriotic and philanthropic public services, as far as possible, in the very words of the subject of his biography. For that purpose, every speech made by Mr. Cobden within the walls of Parliament, and, so far as they could be traced, every utterance of his delivered elsewhere, have been carefully perused. And the principle of selection applied to the citations which have been chosen, has been to supply, not so much (except in a few signal cases) the finest specimens of Cobden's oratory as the passages which are most autobiographical. So far as was possible, in the succeeding pages Cobden has been made to tell the story of his own life.

The Author has to express his indebtedness for much information and insight into the inner and less prominent incidents of Mr. Cobden's life, and shades of his character, to a large number of gentlemen who stood in various degrees of intimacy to the great Free Trade Apostle at the successive epochs of his career. To specify here by name one such contributor to whatever value this book may possess, without mentioning all, would be invidious. The Author, therefore, contents himself with acknowledging in general terms his equal obligations to many kind assistants in his labor of love. Turning to published works, out of very many which have been consulted, Miss Martineau's "History of the Thirty Years' Peace," Mr. Prentice's "History of the Anti-Corn-Law League," and the Reverend Henry Richard's "Life of Joseph Sturge," are among the mines from which the Author has drawn most largely. A copious Index is appended, in which it has been endeavored to give a ready clew to the opinions held by Mr. Cobden on all public questions, and to group around him his associates, whether those who were well known or those who were less conspicuous.

It is hoped that such a book, at a period when the recent political stagnation seems in a degree to be passing away, may be of some benefit to the thoughtful reader. Although not written expressly for young people, if there has been a leading feeling in the Author's mind during its preparation, it has been that, if his book could serve in any degree to induce some members of the rising manhood of the empire to imbibe the contagion of that high ideal of the duties of citizenship which was Cobden's great inspiration, he would at once have laid a not unworthy chaplet on Cobden's tomb, and, after a humble sort, continued Cobden's great work, by enlisting recruits for that army of progress of which he was the chief leader in our days.

Our vignette, representing Cobden's birth-place ere it was altered and extended, is taken from an early volume of the "Illustrated London News," to the proprietors of which historically valuable journal we have to tender our best thanks for permission to reproduce it.

CONTENTS.

LIST OF ILLUSTRATIONS.

[THE SITE OF MR. COBDEN'S GRAVE IS INDICATED BY A CROSS,
ERECTED TO MARK THE GRAVE OF HIS SON, WHICH WILL
BE OBSERVED TO THE LEFT OF A YEW-TREE.]

LIFE OF RICHARD COBDEN.

CHAPTER I.

EARLY DAYS.

One of the daily London newspapers, in its report of the funeral of Mr. Cobden, thus described the general character of the locality of his birth and burial: "There is not, perhaps, a lovelier part of England, a lovelier country, than that part of Sussex in which the now historic village of Midhurst is situated. Hills covered with foliage, valleys bright with verdure or teeming with fertility, alternate with dark, sombre-looking heaths, sandy patches, and trim, silent, old-fashioned villages, and isolated farm-houses built in the days of the Tudors." All authorities whom we have consulted bear similar testimony to the beauteous old-world character of the neighborhood. Even when Cobbet, in his "Rural Rides," strikes into the Weald of Sussex, on the confines of the western portion of which Midhurst stands, upon a slight eminence above the River Rother, he lays aside his customary style of denunciation, and thus eulogizes the locality: "There is no misery to be seen here; I have seen no wretchedness in Sussex; nothing to be at all compared to that which I have seen in other parts; and as to these villages in the South Downs, they are beautiful to behold. There is an appearance of comfort about the dwellings of the laborers that is very pleasant to behold. The gardens are neat, and full of vegetables of the best kinds. I saw with great delight a pig at almost every laborer's door."

The neighborhood abounds in the splendid ancestral residences of the noble and untitled families of Richmond, Camoys, Egmont, the Percies, the Montagues, and the Wyndhams; and is also thickly studded with fine old-timbered farms and manor-houses, which bespeak the woody wealth of the ancient oak forests. Many old-descended yeomen's families are preserved; the Entyknapps of Pockford, for example, hold by a tenure dating from the Saxon times. It was at Cowdray, the ancient seat of the Montagues, now a picturesque ruin, but habitable when Dr. Johnson paid a visit to it from Brighton, that that sage said to Boswell, "Sir, I should like to stay here four-and-twenty hours. We see here how our ancestors lived." Here, nearly two centuries before, Queen Elizabeth visited the great Lord Montague, one of her heroes of the Armada. Here, with a cross-bow, she killed three or four deer as they were driven past her sylvan bower; the Countess of

Kildare, with the true sagacity of the Geraldines, taking care to bring down only one. Verdley Castle, which lies to the north of Midhurst, was "known," in Camden's days, "only to those that hunt the marten cat."

The personal associations of the neighborhood are not less interesting and seductive. Otway was born at Verdley; Charles Fox sat for Midhurst before Cobden was born; and while he was yet in early childhood, Sir Charles Lyell was receiving, at the grammar-school of the quaint, old-gabled borough, the rudiments of his education.

At the farm-house of Dunford, a short distance from Midhurst, and a view of which forms the subject of the vignette on our title-page, Richard Cobden first drew breath on the 3d of June, 1804. His father farmed his own land, a holding of moderate extent. He had been for a short time resident in Midhurst, as also had his father before him. The latter, we believe, discharged the duties of chief magistrate of the little town. In Midhurst, Cobden received the rudiments of his education. The grammar-school where he was educated at one time enjoyed a high reputation, but its endowment being no more than nominal, we believe that it has fallen into decay. Within the last year or two attempts have been made to reinstate it in somewhat of its old position. Of these efforts Mr. Cobden, in the concluding portion of his life, was one of the chief promoters.

A comparatively small sum—from a thousand to fifteen hundred pounds—would suffice to attain this object. We can not help thinking, and expressing here the opinion, that no public memorial of Mr. Cobden's services and merits would be more eminently appropriate and honoring to his memory than the completion of this good work, one of the last he had at heart.

At an early period of the boy's life his father died; and the youth, being taken under the guardianship of an uncle who was a London warehouse-man, repaired to London to seek his fortunes in his relative's establishment. From this he appears shortly to have removed himself to another house in the same department of trade, where he drew attention by his eagerness to acquire information, and the variety of his reading. His master, a man belonging to the old school, and steeped in the prejudices of the time, warned him against so much reading, telling him he would be certain, if he persisted in the indulgence, to spoil his prospects for life. We need not say how this prediction was falsified. The master lived to fail in his business, and to see the youth he had employed at the head of a prosperous and money-making firm. Cobden did not resent the ill-advised, but doubtless well-meant, attempt at restraint. He allowed his old employer a sufficient annual allowance, which was regularly paid until the date of the old man's death.

Hitherto Cobden's employment had been confined to the indoor routine of a warehouse. At an early age he embarked upon the more varied and exciting calling of a commercial traveler, commencing his duties in that capacity at a very modest rate of remuneration. In fact, it was only by accident—being asked to assume the duties of a traveler who had fallen sick—that he was transferred from the warehouse, or counting-house, to the " road." In his new sphere he soon made himself exceedingly popular, and equally profitable as a representative of the house that employed him. He sent home large orders; and many men yet living, and still engaged in trade, recall with pleasure the frank and affable, though modest and diffident, manner of Cobden in the after-dinner talk—and sometimes disputation—of the commercial room. Already he was deeply versed in Adam Smith, and he was a peripatetic and enthusiastic advocate of thorough-going Free Trade. With half jocularity and half seriousness, he proposed the establishment of a " Smithian Society," on the model of the Linnæan and similar associations devoted to natural science, for the then much-needed purpose of elucidating and disseminating the opinions of the great master of political economy.

In course of time the firm which he represented withdrew from business, and disposed of their interest and good-will to certain of their more energetic *employés*. Among these was Cobden. A correspondent of the *Manchester Courier*, writing a few days after Mr. Cobden's death, thus narrates the circumstances of his first independent start in business: " Mr. Cobden began life as a lad in a London warehouse. Growing into a young man, he was sent on matters of business to many of the houses with which his firm was connected. Among those he so visited was Mr. John Lewis, of 101 Oxford Street. Mr. Lewis conceived a liking for the young man on account of the smart and business-like manner in which he used to come to his house and transact whatever he had to do, and often gave him a few kind words. One day young Cobden came to him, and with some hesitation told him that he and two of his comrades, young men like himself, had heard of a business near Manchester, which a gentleman was retiring from, and the plant of which was to be had for £1500; this sum the three had agreed to raise among them, but Cobden had no friends to help him with his quota, and therefore he would venture to ask Mr. Lewis if he would do so. Mr. Lewis, from his partiality to him, at once assented, and Cobden left him in high spirits. But soon after he called again, with a long face, to say his colleagues had not been able to raise their £500 each. After a while, however, he came again, to state that the owner of the business in question, having heard favorably of the trio, agreed to let them have it for Mr. Cobden's £500. Would Mr. Lewis still let him have the money? Mr. Lewis very kindly complied, and the three shortly after began the world together. The £500 was speedily repaid; and, after a very few years, one and then another of the partners drew out of the business with a handsome fortune, and Richard Cobden came to be what he was. The foregoing particulars were related to the writer by Mr. Lewis, who retired from business about twenty-five years ago, and subsequently died in Madeira." The new firm had three establishments: one at Sabden, near Clitheroe, for the printing of the calicoes in which they dealt, under the title of Sheriff, Foster, & Co.; and two others for the sale of their goods—one in London, termed Sheriff, Gillet, & Co., and another in Manchester, under the personal management of Mr. Cobden, and entitled Richard Cobden & Co. It was in the year 1830, when he had only reached his twenty-sixth year, that Cobden took up his residence in Manchester, and commenced business on his own account. His warehouse was in Mozley Street, which hitherto had been the Saville Row of Manchester, consisting entirely of the houses of medical men and other private residences. We believe that it is now entirely composed of warehouses; but Cobden & Co.'s was the first to intrude on its privacy, and inaugurate the transmutation, which is now complete.

The fortunes of the house rapidly progressed. "The custom of the calico trade," says one of the authorities from whom these particulars are derived, "at that period was to print a few designs, and watch cautiously and carefully those which were most acceptable to the public, when large quantities of those which seemed to be preferred were printed off and offered to the retail dealer. Mr. Cobden introduced a new mode of business. Possessed of great taste, of excellent tact, and remarkable knowledge of the trade in all its details, he and his partners did not follow the cautious and slow policy of their predecessors, but fixing themselves upon the best designs, they had these printed off at once, and pushed the sale energetically throughout the country. Those pieces which failed to take in the home market were at once shipped to other countries, and the consequence was that the associated firms became very prosperous." Cobden took long and extended foreign journeys, both in the old world and the new, to open up markets for his prints. These journeys had also political and literary results, to which reference will be made in succeeding pages. "Cobden's prints" became very fashionable. After he had become a great public man, the wives and dependents of the great landowners, whose monopoly he assailed, were seen in public clad in his garments; and, at the heat of the agitation, the young Queen Victoria herself was observed, by the passengers by the newly-opened Great Western Railway, strolling on the slopes of Windsor Park plainly dressed in one of "Cobden's prints."

In Manchester, Cobden early entered upon public life. Such a man could not fail to be strongly affected by the ideas prevalent, and the forces in conflict, at the period of the great Reform struggle. The circumstances of his first introduction into the arena of local and general politics are thus narrated by Mr. Cathrall, one of the proprietors and editors of the *Manchester Times:*

"While my late partner and myself were earnestly engaged as journalists, now about thirty years back, in the severe struggle then entered upon by the inhabitants of Manchester for obtaining the incorporation of the town, we received a series of letters upon that and other subjects of public interest from an anonymous correspondent under the signature of 'Libra.' These letters, which were generally furnished alternate weeks, were marked by so much thought and ability that we were desirous to have an interview with the writer, and accordingly inserted a line in our paper to that effect, mentioning a time for the purpose. About noon the same day that this notice appeared, the publisher of our paper notified to me that a gentleman in the outer office wished to see me, when the stranger, on being invited into my private room, introduced himself as Richard Cobden. His person and name being alike unknown to me, and not recollecting for the moment that a stranger was expected in accordance with the notice inserted in our journal, I begged he would inform me of the object of his call, when he said he was 'Libra;' adding, 'I observe from your paper that you wish to see me.' We at once became great friends. Soon after, poor Prentice, my partner, entered the room, and on being informed that it was 'Libra' who was with me, warmly shook him by the hand, and at the same time complimented him on the skill, etc., displayed in his letters.

"We gathered that he was engaged in business in Mozley Street; that he had only recently come to Manchester, and had but few acquaintances there.

"I well remember that in this interview he was very diffident, and somewhat nervous in temperament; at the same time, it was obvious to us, even then, that he was in ability and promise much above the average stamp of young men.

"It happening that a public meeting, under the presidency of Mr. Prentice, in furtherance of the incorporation of Manchester, was to be held that same evening at the Cotton Free Tavern, in Ancoats (a favorite political rendezvous of the period referred to), my partner at once solicited Mr. Cobden to accompany him and take part in the proceedings.

"Although so many years have passed since, I well recollect that Mr. Cobden declined to attend the meeting; in fact, he evidently shrunk from the task of speaking on the occasion, and it was not until repeatedly pressed to do so that he consented, although the meeting was quite of a minor character.

"'I assure you,' he said, 'I never yet made a speech of any description, excepting, perhaps, an after-dinner one at a commercial table.' Having at length obtained the promise of his attendance, it was arranged that he should take his tea at our office on the way to the meeting, which he accordingly did.

"After the opening speech of the chairman, he called upon Mr. Cobden to move the first resolution, introducing him as his young friend, who had recently contributed to the *Manchester Times* the able letters signed 'Libra.' His speech, however, on this occasion was a signal failure. He was nervous, confused, and, in fact, practically broke down, and the chairman had to apologize for him, but at the same time expressed full confidence as to the success and usefulness of his future career.

"Such was Mr. Cobden's *début* before the Manchester public as a speaker. So far as his own feelings were concerned, for some time he was so discouraged by his maiden effort that I am pretty confident, had this lamented and remarkable man, whose oratory subsequently was of so persuasive a kind, been allowed to follow the bent of his inclination, he never again would have appeared as a public speaker.

"Our professional acquaintance with Mr. Cobden, thus formed, led to his introduction to the political circles of Manchester, and in a short period he took an active part in most public matters affecting the interests of the town, and was chosen one of the first members of the corporation, whose charter he materially assisted in obtaining."

Mr. Cobden was not deterred by this oratorical failure from again attempting to acquire by practice facility of public speech. He must have progressed rapidly, for we find that upon the opening of the Manchester Athenæum, the establishment of which was effected in spite of great, and at one time apparently insurmountable difficulties—which Cobden is stated more than all other men put together to have overcome—he was chosen to deliver the inaugural address. In connection with the movement for the extension of municipal insititutions of a modern and liberal character to Manchester, he published a terse pamphlet, entitled "Incorporate your Borough," in which the vices and jobbery of the existing system were vigorously exposed. He also made frequent appearances in Manchester, and elsewhere in the neighborhood, in behalf of the dawning movement for national education. It was in connection with this movement that John Bright and Richard Cobden became personally acquainted. Altogether, "Mr. Alderman Cobden" had become a man of decided local mark, and a man of whom great hopes were entertained by his intimates, and by his coadjutors in public causes, by the time he was about thirty or thirty-one years of age.

CHAPTER II.

FIRST PERIOD OF THE ANTI-CORN-LAW AGITATION.

MANCHESTER, which now stands so identified with a school of politicians which subordinates all other considerations to a paramount policy of freedom of trade, was one of the boroughs enfranchised by the Reform Bill of 1832. At the general election of that year, the Manchester men returned two members completely pledged to this course of legislation. Mr. Mark Phillips, in his canvass, declared himself decidedly opposed to "the East India, the Bank, and the timber monopolies, and that greatest of all monopolies which was upheld by the Corn Laws." Mr. Poulett Thompson, afterward Lord Sydenham, who held the office of Vice-President, and afterward of President, of the Board of Trade in Lord Grey's administration, was known to be in advance of most of his colleagues in his general political opinions, and of all of them on questions of commercial reform. He was selected by the Manchester Liberals as their second candidate; and he and Mr. Phillips were elected by considerable majorities over the other candidates—William Cobbet, one of the great family of the Hopes,

and the present Lord Overstone. From that date
Manchester became the avowed and acknowledged head-quarters of the Free Trade party. It
was not long before certain of the leading men in
the locality began to take the first steps, which
led, as ultimate result, to the formation of the
Anti-Corn-Law League. In January, 1834, a
meeting of merchants and manufacturers was
held. Good speeches were made, but little came
of the meeting, the members of which carefully
disclaimed all intention of forming any association. Meanwhile, in Parliament, Mr. Hume was
urging the views of the Free-Traders, receiving
support from snch of the Whigs as Poulett
Thompson, the late Lord Carlisle, and the present
Lord Grey. But the monopolists mustered in
force, and defeated Mr. Hume's very moderate
proposal, which only contemplated the substitu-
tion of a fixed for a fluctuating duty on corn. The
country, too, was apathetic, for trade was prosperous and food cheap. Mr. Thompson, however,
succeeded in introducing some valuable amendments ere the dissolution of the first administration of Lord Melbourne, and he fairly merits the
statement that " he occupied, beneficially to the
public, the time between the death of Huskisson
and the advent of Cobden." He abolished the
duty on hemp, considerably reduced the taxes on
dye-stuffs and medicines, and made a large and advantageous simplification of the tariff generally.

The harvest of 1835 was gloriously abundant, and in the first meeting of the reconstituted Melbourne ministry, after the short Peel interregnum, with the Houses of Parliament, they were assailed by the landowners with the usual cries of the " distress" inflicted upon the agricultural interest by the abundance of the crops. The plenty still kept the people apathetic. An old Scotchwoman, when some one was endeavoring to impress upon her the then prevalent delusion that the higher prices were, the better would be the condition of farm laborers, replied, " Na, na; ye'll no persuade me that when there's plenty o' meal puir folks will get less than when it's scarce." The people had plenty in 1835, and that plenty begat a certain political improvidence. They were deaf to the considerations addressed to them by the Free Trade pioneers—that this cheapness was most precarious, absolutely depending, so long as the Corn Laws remained, upon the chance of a succession of similarly plentiful harvests.

It was just at this era that Cobden, who had been, ever since he emerged from boyhood, training himself, by the most omnivorous reading, extended travel, and careful thought, for the public position he was providentially designed to occupy, enrolled himself openly among the Free Traders. He worked first, and anonymously, with his pen ere his voice was heard. The following passage from Mr. Prentice's "History of the Anti-Corn-Law League" describes Cobden's first enlistment in the Free Trade ranks. We present Mr. Prentice's version of his first acquaintance with Mr. Cobden entire, as we have given that of Mr. Cathrall in the preceding chapter, leaving our readers to determine for themselves which seems the more worthy of credit. Our own preference decidedly leans to Mr. Cathrall's, as being more self-consistent and probable upon the face of it. It is hardly necessary to state our belief that the discrepancies, signal though they be, arise from simple forgetfulness on the part of one or both of the narrators.

"In 1835 there had been sent to me for publication in my paper some admirably-written letters. They contained no internal evidence to guide me in guessing as to who might be the writer, and I concluded that there was some new man among us, who, if he held a station that would enable him to take a part in public affairs, would exert a widely beneficial influence among us. He might be some young man in a warehouse, who had thought deeply on political economy, and its practical application in our commercial policy, who might not be soon in a position to come before the public as an influential teacher; but we had, I had no doubt, somewhere among us, perhaps sitting solitary after his day's work in some obscure apartment, like Adam Smith in his

quiet closet at Kirkcaldy, one inwardly and quietly conscious of his power, but patiently biding
his time to popularize the doctrines set forth in
the 'Wealth of Nations,' and to make the multitude think as the philosopher had thought, and
to act upon their convictions. I told many that
a new man had come, and the question was often
put among my friends, 'Who is he?' It is some
satisfaction to me now, writing seventeen years
after that period, that I had anticipated the deliberate verdict of the nation. In the course of
that year, a pamphlet, published by Ridgway,
under the title 'England, Ireland, and America,'
was put into my hand by a friend, inscribed 'From
the Author,' and I instantly recognized the hand-
writing of my unknown, much by me desired to
be known, correspondent; and I was greatly
gratified when I learned that Mr. Cobden, the
author of the pamphlet, desired to meet me at
my friend's house. I went with something of the
same kind of feelings which I had experienced
when I first, four years before, went to visit Jer-
emy Bentham, the father of the practical Free
Traders; nor was I disappointed except in one
respect. I found a man who could enlighten by
his knowledge, counsel by his prudence, and con-
ciliate by his temper and manners, and who, if
he found his way into the House of Commons,
would secure its respectful attention; but I had
been an actor among men who, from 1812 to 1832,

had fought in the rough battle for Parliamentary Reform, and I missed, in the unassuming gentleman before me, not the energy, but the apparent hardihood and dash which I had, forgetting the change of times, believed to be requisites to the success of a popular leader. In after years, and after, having attained great platform popularity, he had been elected a member of Parliament, and when men sneered and said he would soon find his level there, as other mob orators had done, I ventured to say that he would be in his proper vocation there, and that his level would be among the first men of the House."

The pamphlet which (according to Mr. Prentice) thus formed the occasion of the introduction of the leader of the League to its historian, really assumes the proportions of a book. We are reluctantly compelled to resist the temptation of summarizing this the first considerable production of Cobden's pen. It was from first to last a protest against the Palmerstonian foreign policy, and represented views from which Cobden never in his after life in the slightest iota swerved, and which he never ceased to present to the nation, uninfluenced by the fair weather of popularity, undeterred by the foul weather of temporary seasons of alienation, when England was in one of its intermittent war fevers. These opening sentences from the preface are remarkably characteristic of the man, and are of universal application in English history—as pertinent in 1865 as they were in 1835.

"The following pages were written principally with a view to endeavor to prove the erroneous foreign policy of the government of this country. English statesmen of every age, down even to the present day, have one and all lost sight of that distinguishing and privileged feature which is peculiar to the insular situation of Great Britain. If we go back to the year 1805, when Nelson destroyed the remains of the French navy at Trafalgar, these islands were thenceforth as secure against foreign molestation as though they had formed a portion of the moon's territory; yet from that time down to 1815 we waged incessant war, and incurred four hundred millions of debt for interests purely continental. Our European commerce yields but a poor set-off against the expenses of the war. The hundred days of Napoleon cost us forty millions, the interest of which at five per cent. is two millions. Now, our exports to all Europe, of British manufactures, amount to about eighteen millions annually; and, taking the profit at ten per cent., it falls short of two millions; so that all the profit of all our merchants, trading with all Europe, will not yield sufficient to pay the yearly interest of the cost of the last one hundred days' war on the Continent, leaving all the other hundreds of millions spent previously as so much dead loss."

Cobden came again before the public as an author in 1836. In that year, Tait, of Edinburg, republished in a cheap form four articles which Cobden had contributed to *Tait's Magazine*, written with the design of allaying the Russophobia then prevalent, which Mr. Urquhart and his school (not, it was believed by some, without the complicity of the Foreign Secretary) had endeavored to excite in the country. This pamphlet, like the other, is an admirable product of Cobden's clear and vigorous intellect. A few selected sentences will suffice to justify our statement.

"They who, pointing to the chart of Russia, shudder at her expanse of impenetrable forests, her wastes of eternal snow, her howling wildernesses, frowning mountains, and solitary rivers ; or they who stand aghast at her boundless extent of fertile but uncultivated steppes, her millions of serfs, and her towns the abodes of poverty and filth, know nothing of the true origin, in modern and future times, of national power and greatness. This question admits of an appropriate illustration by putting the names of a couple of heroes of Russian aggression and violence in contrast with two of their contemporaries, the champions of improvement in England. At the very period when Potemkin and Suwarrow were engaged in effecting their important Russian conquests in Poland and the Crimea, and while these monsters of carnage were filling the world with

C

the lustre of their fame, and lighting up one half
of Europe with the conflagrations of war—two
obscure individuals, the one an optician and the
other a barber, both equally disregarded by the
chroniclers of the day, were quietly gaining vic-
tories in the realms of science, which have produced a more abundant harvest of wealth and
power to their native country than has been ac-
quired by all the wars of Russia during the last
two centuries. Those illustrious commanders in
the war of improvement, Watt and Arkwright,
with a band of subalterns—the thousand ingenious and practical discoverers who have followed
in their train—have, with their armies of artisans,
conferred a power and consequence upon England, springing from successive triumphs in the
physical sciences and the mechanical arts, and
wholly independent of territorial increase—compared with which, all that she owes to the evanescent exploits of her warrior heroes shrinks into
insignificance and obscurity. If we look into fu-
turity, and speculate upon the probable career of
one of these inventions, may we not with safety
predict that the steam-engine—the perfecting of
which belongs to our own age, and which even
now is exerting an influence in the four quarters
of the globe—will at no distant day produce moral
and physical changes all over the world of a magnitude and permanency surpassing the effects of
all the wars and conquests which have convulsed

mankind since the beginning of time? England owes to the peaceful exploits of Watt and Arkwright, and not to the deeds of Nelson and Wellington, her commerce, which now extends to every corner of the earth, and which casts into comparative obscurity, by the grandeur and extent of its operations, the peddling ventures of Tyre, Carthage, and Venice, confined within the limits of an inland sea."

The following is no poor specimen of the quick, incisive thrust with which Cobden so often stabbed and burst the bubbles of many popular delusions: "The writers who have attempted to lead public opinion upon the subject have not scrupled to claim the interposition of our government with Russia for the purpose of restoring to *freedom* and *independence* those Caucasian tribes to which we have before alluded as being under the partial dominion of Russia. Their previous state of freedom may be appreciated when we recollect that within our own time a fierce war was waged between the most powerful of these nations (the Georgians) and the Turks in consequence of their having refused to continue to supply the harems of the latter with a customary annual tribute of the handsomest of their daughters; offering, however, at the same time, in lieu, a yearly contribution in money."

In 1836, an Anti-Corn-Law Association was formed in London; but it proposed little in the way of organization and agitation, and did not represent a very numerous constituency. Nevertheless, it comprised the names of many very valuable public men; among others, Joseph Brotherton, Silk Buckingham, William Clay, Thomas Duncombe, William Ewart, George Grote, Joseph Hume, Sir William Molesworth, Mr. Roebuck, Mr. Scholefield, Colonel Thompson, Mr. Wakley, Ebenezer Elliot, William Howitt, Place, the Westminster tailor, Prentice, the future historian of the League, Colonel Leicester Stanhope, Tait, the Radical publisher; and as representatives of literature, Laman Blanchard and Thomas Campbell. This association at least kept the question of Corn Law Repeal before the public until it was replaced by the formation of the League.

1837 was a year of great commercial depression. There were heavy failures in London, Liverpool, Manchester, and Glasgow. Ere the summer arrived, deep distress had reached the homes of the working classes. In Lancashire, thousands of factory hands were discharged. The Chartist agitation was undertaken, and much sedition openly expressed. During the panic, which was not of long continuance, the belief spread that it might not have occurred at all if the nation had been permitted to enjoy a regular importation of corn. Mr. Clay moved in the House of Commons for a fixed duty of 10s. on wheat. Among his supporters of the Whig ranks were Lords Howick and

Morpeth, Sir George Grey, Sir Henry Parnell, and Mr. Labouchere. The death of the king causing an election, Manchester's Anti-Corn-Law members were returned by large majorities over Mr. Gladstone, senior. Other Lancashire towns returned Free Traders. Mr. Cobden was traveling on the Continent. In his absence he was proposed for Stockport, and was within a very few votes of being returned. In all, thirty-eight Free Traders were returned for constituencies numbering five millions of souls. In counties and the smaller boroughs, where much flagrant bribery and corruption had been brought into action, the Protectionists had it their own way, and loudly vaunted the alleged, but suborned, reaction in their favor. A banquet was given to Mr. Brotherton to celebrate his return for Salford. Mr. Cobden, who had returned from his foreign journey, was present, and delivered an admirable speech, the chief gist of which was a recommendation of the ballot, showing how different would have been the result of the general election if the electors had been so protected.

Mr. Cobden now endeavored to induce the Manchester Chamber of Commerce to organize a decided Anti-Corn-Law agitation. Its members, however, while repeating the protest against the Corn Laws which they had made ten years before, refused to organize any more active measures of aggression. More than once during this year the subject was brought before the House of Commons by Mr. Villiers and others, but the great majority of members would hardly even listen. The Marquis of Chandos thus coolly demanded the continuance of the chronic robbery of labor by the landowners: "The agricultural interest is now enjoying some little respite from the distress of past years, and all it asks for is peace and quietness, and that it shall not be inconvenienced by legislative enactments of any kind." In the course of one of the debates, Lord Melbourne made a memorable and important declaration: he said, "The government would not take a decided part till it was certain the majority of the people were in favor of a change." This was a direct invitation and challenge to organized agitation; physical events, too, fanned the progress of opinion. The summer was wet. In August, wheat was at 72s., just double its price after the harvest of two years previously. Such men as Colonel Thompson and Joseph Sturge redoubled their efforts, and many of the newspapers which had been lukewarm showed a growing bias to conversion.

In September of this year Dr. Bowring was entertained at a public dinner in Blackburn. Mr. Prentice seized the occasion of his expected passage through Manchester to issue circulars to a number of the more decided local Free Traders to meet the doctor, who had just returned to England from the Continent and Egypt, where he had been engaged in a mission for the promotion of freer commercial intercourse. About sixty gentlemen met together, and the meeting was very enthusiastic. Dr. Bowring denounced the Corn Laws in unmeasured terms. "It is impossible," said he, "to estimate the amount of human misery created by the Corn Laws, or the amount of human pleasure overthrown by them. In every part of the world I have found the plague-spot." In the course of the evening a Mr. Howie proposed, after the enthusiasm of the meeting had been very thoroughly evoked, "that the present company at once form themselves into an Anti-Corn-Law Association." The proposal was warmly entertained, and the succeeding Monday arranged for a meeting formally to consider the project. It was agreed that the association should agitate for no half measures, but direct its assaults against *any and every corn law.* A Provisional Committee was formed, and announced by public advertisement. Mr. Cobden's name appeared in the second list of committee-men advertised. They subscribed among themselves nearly £11,000; and, as a first step, appointed Mr. Paulton, a young medical student of the highest qualifications, to deliver popular lectures on the subject wherever he could get a hearing. He broke ground in Manchester. The first sentences of his first lecture clearly and without any equivocation declared the fundamental principle of the association. "It has been established on the same righteous principle as the Anti-Slavery Society. The object of that society was to obtain the free right for the negroes to possess their own flesh and blood—the object of this is to obtain the free right of the people to exchange their labor for as much food as can be got for it; that we may no longer be obliged by law to buy our food at one shop, and that the dearest in the world, but be at liberty to go to that at which it can be obtained cheapest." At the conclusion of a second lecture in Manchester, Mr. Paulton quoted these lines, which were received with the utmost enthusiasm. Many hundreds of times afterward were they cited at League meetings. Their so frequent citation forms part of the history of the League; we therefore insert them:

"For what were all these landed patriots born?
  To hunt, and vote, and raise the price of corn.
  Safe in their barns, these Sabine tillers sent
  Your brethren out to battle. Why? For rent!
  Year after year they voted cent. per cent. ;
  Blood, sweat, and tear-wrung millions! Why? For rent!
  They roared, they dined, they drank, they swore, they meant
  To die for England. Why then live? For rent!
  And will they not repay the treasures lent?
  No! down with every thing, and up with rent!
  Their good, ill, health, wealth, joy, or discontent,
  Being, end, aim, religion—rent, rent, rent!"

Requests at once poured in from great and small towns for lectures by Mr. Paulton, and his

success was equally indicated by the abuse show-
ered upon him by the landlord papers.

The enthusiasm was reflected upon the Manchester Chamber of Commerce. A general meeting of its members, held in December, was the
largest that had ever assembled. They resolved
to petition Parliament for total repeal, and very
properly one gentleman, while he stigmatized the
Corn Law legislation as "one of most shameful
injustice," stated that "they were not so unjust
and inconsistent as to ask any protection for
manufactures." The bulk of the meeting were
barely ripe for this. Nor is this to be wondered
at, for probably there never was a delusion in the
whole history of human error so difficult to expel
from the heads of men, and especially of *classes* of
men, as the supposed advantages of protective or
prohibitory legislation. Cobden was present, and
at once threw his weight into the large and liberal
view. From his very argumentative speech we
extract these sentences, which prove that he, at
least, had nothing to learn from the very first of
the maxims of the Free Trade gospel—that it was
any and all protection, and not the mere protection of the landed interest, that he assailed:

"In a country such as this, where a boundless
extent of capital is yielding only three or four per
cent., it is folly to suppose that by any artificial
means any *trade* can long be made to pay more
than the average rate of profit. The effect of all

such restrictions will only be to narrow the field of industry, and thus, in the end, to injure instead of benefiting the parties intended to be protected. But look at the very opposite position in which the owners of land stand. I will suppose that a law could be passed to raise the price of wheat to a thousand shillings a bushel; now what would be the effect of this but that the capitalists, who now get their ten per cent. profit in London or Manchester, would immediately urge their sons to bid fifty per cent. over the farmers of Norfolk; and if these were still in the way of getting higher profits than other trades, then other competitors would appear to bid fifty per cent. over them, until Mr. Coke's farms had reached the full market price, and yielded only the ordinary rate of profit of all other trades. But mark the difference in the situation of the landowner and the calico-printer: while additional mills and print-works might be erected to meet the demand for calicoes and prints, not an acre of land could be added to the present domains of the aristocracy, and therefore every shilling of protection on corn must pass into the pockets of the landowners, without at all benefiting the tenant or the agricultural laborer; whereas, on the other hand, no extent of protection could possibly benefit the manufacturer." He concluded his speech by submitting a resolution proposing a petition for the abolition of all protective duties whatsoever.

The meeting was adjourned for a week. In the interval the municipal charter of incorporation had been granted to Manchester. At the adjourned meeting Mr. Cobden appeared as Mr. Alderman Cobden, having been elevated to that civic rank by the inhabitants of one of the wards. Mr. Cobden's motion was carried by a large majority, and so important a body as the Chamber of Commerce of the cotton metropolis thereby committed to absolute Free Trade. The discussions had created great interest, and were widely reported in the country. Cobden was from this day known to all England as a Free Trade champion.

The Anti-Corn-Law Association now determined to prosecute their work with augmented vigor, and to make large pecuniary contributions with that object. A meeting was held in January, 1839, at which, among other proposals, "Mr. Alderman Cobden recommended an investment of a part of the property of the gentlemen present to save the rest from confiscation." A short extract from the newspaper report of the day is enough to indicate the determinedness which had now taken possession of the minds of these early Free Traders.

"The chairman said that, though young in business, he would put down £50 (cheers).

"Mr. J. B. Smith would give £100, and he was commissioned to put down Mr. Schuster's name for £100 (cheers).

" Alderman Cobden said he would give £100 (cheers).

" Mr. J. C. Dyer would give £100 most cheerfully, and £1000 more if it were wanted (cheers).

" Mr. W. Rawson said he could only give £50 now, but would give half of all he possessed if it were needed (cheers)."

Before leaving the room £1800 was subscribed, and large additional subscriptions were speedily announced. In a few days the total exceeded £6000.

Meanwhile the Chartists, under Feargus O'Connor, had commenced their obstructive policy of denouncing the Anti-Corn-Law movement as only intended to advantage the manufacturers by enabling them to purchase labor at reduced rates; or, while admitting the desirability of Corn-Law Repeal, alleging that its consideration ought to be postponed until a complete suffrage had been secured. Tories also came forward to disturb Mr. Paulton's lectures and other Free Trade meetings by the former pretext. It became pretty obvious that certain Chartist leaders acted with singular conformity of plan and purpose with that pursued by such Tory obstructives, and it began to be more than suspected that the identity of policy was more than accidental. Other associations were springing up besides that of Manchester. At a dinner given in that city to the members of Parliament who had voted with Mr. Villiers on his Anti-Corn-Law motion in Parliament, Mr. Cobden took advantage of the presence of representatives from all the principal towns of England and Scotland to suggest that a general central association of the associations (so to speak) should be formed. This was favorably entertained, and was the first suggestion to make the agitation a combined national one—a decided step toward the League. A meeting of delegates from the various towns was appointed to be held on the 4th of February, in London, at a hotel within a stone's throw of the House of Commons. These delegates had an interview with Lord Melbourne, and, through Mr. Villiers, prayed to be heard at the bar of the House in support of that gentleman's annual motion. But their plaint was of course refused. The delegates held a meeting at Brown's Hotel, at which they met a large number of metropolitan Free Traders ere they returned to their respective homes. Cobden said " he thought there was no cause for despondency because the House over the way refused to hear them. They were the representatives of three millions of the people—they were the evidence that the great towns had banded themselves together, and their alliance would be a Hanseatic League against the feudal Corn Law plunderers. The castles which crowned the rocks along the Rhine, the Danube, and the Elbe, had once been the strong-hold of feudal oppressors, but they had

been dismantled by a league; and they now only
adorned the landscape as picturesque memorials
of the past, while the people below had lost all
fear of plunder, and tilled their vineyards in
peace." Some of the London Free Traders invited the delegates to a public dinner at one of
the theatres. But they declined the invitation—
they were going back to their head-quarters at
Manchester to concert farther measures.

Shortly after their return to Manchester, a
meeting, convened by the Free Trade party, was
with great riot and violence broken up by a mob,
using the names of Richard Oastler and O'Connor
as their war cries, and led by certain drunken and
dirty Irishmen of the laboring class. After this
the heads of the movement resolved that only
members of the association and persons to whom
tickets of entrance were given should be admitted to the meetings. A few days after, Cobden
addressed a large assembly admitted by ticket;
and after denouncing in terms of manly indignation the conduct of the rioters, he addressed these
words of appropriate warning to the working
men: " Working men of Manchester, look to
yourselves, you who look to your benefit and sick
clubs, and your trade societies—look to those
men who would take forcible possession of this
room, which was occupied by the Anti-Corn-Law
Association—who had upset meetings called to
form Parthenons and other literary associations

—who would make violent inroads upon Anti-Slavery meetings ; these men will take possession of your meetings unless you check them in the bud. Nay, more; I have no hesitation in saying that even your quiet, happy, and well-regulated firesides will not be safe unless the strong arm of the law is brought to interfere between you and the wishes of those lawless men, who have no other restraint but the fear of the law and its consequences."

A friend and associate of Cobden at that period of his career at which we have now arrived thus describes the impression he then formed of him :

" Many years of political turmoil have passed away since we first saw Richard Cobden. He was then a comparatively young man. . . . . In private.life we never met a more loveable man than Richard Cobden. He was mildness, and gentleness, and sympathetic courtesy personified. The natural refinement and modesty of his mind was visible in his countenance and in his whole deportment. He had the happy art of drawing people about him, and of so making them his personal friends by the interest he took in them, and by the certainty with which he inspired them, that his best advice was ever at their service. No one meeting Mr. Cobden for the first time, and under any circumstances, would experience any difficulty in addressing him. There

was that in his very look which inspired confidence, and in his manner which conciliated more
than passing good-will. He affected no superiority, and claimed no deference, even when in
communication with the poorest of the people.
Nothing was easier to see than that Mr. Cobden
thoroughly and heartily sympathized with the
working classes, and that he was constantly employed in devising how he could best assist in
elevating them in the social scale without injury
to the best interests of those above them."

CHAPTER III.

FORMATION OF THE LEAGUE.

THE delegated Free Traders came to the conclusion that the constituencies and the country would require a great deal more of instruction and arousing ere repeal could be extorted from the monopolist Legislature. They issued an address to the public, containing, among other recommendations, the following: "The formation of a permanent union, to be called the ANTI-CORN-LAW LEAGUE, composed of all the towns and districts represented in the delegation, and as many others as might be induced to form Anti-Corn-Law Associations, and to join the League.

"With the view to secure the unity of action, the central office of the League shall be established in Manchester, to which body shall be intrusted, among other duties, that of engaging and recommending competent lecturers, the obtaining the co-operation of the public press, and the establishing and conducting of a stamped circular, for the purpose of keeping a constant correspondence with the local associations."

This manifesto issued, the delegates at once dispersed themselves among their several towns, and held meetings in every part of the country. The League commenced also a vigorous publication of appropriate popular pamphlets, the well-known "Facts for Farmers" being among the first issued. Ten thousand of each sheet were at first issued. Subsequently, in the heat and height of the controversy, an issue of half a million of one pamphlet was far from rare. Within a month of the formation of the League, the "Anti-Corn-Law Circular" was started, and commenced with a circulation of 15,000.

Cobden, of course, was just the man to support such wise and beneficial measures as Rowland Hill's Penny Postage and Lytton Bulwer's reduction on the Taxes on Knowledge. Accordingly, Ashurst and Charles Knight in London did not support these measures with a whit more activity than Cobden and others of the Leaguers displayed in Manchester. Cobden saw that the Free Trade cause would be enormously benefited by these reductions. The "Anti-Corn-Law Circular" was at first issued unstamped, but the government looked upon it as a newspaper, and it had to be stamped. The stamp duty had, by a most propitious accident, been just reduced to a penny. And the stamping of the "Circular" turned out to be most advantageous; for each copy issued, after being handed from one to another, was reposted, generally to some friend in the country, who similarly circulated it in his circle, and thus the very machinery of government became the winged Mercury of the Leaguers who were assailing it. Shortly after came the Penny Postage. It caused the correspondence of the League to increase—literally, we do not use a mere figure of rhetoric—a hundred fold. Banquets seem to have been very much in vogue in the early days of the League. Mr. Paulton, having returned to Lancashire after a most successful tour in Scotland, was entertained at dinner at Bolton. Mr. Cobden was present, and so also was Mr. Bright, then a very young man. Both of them spoke, Mr. Bright's speech being the first delivered by him out of his native town. The occasion is interesting as being the first on which these trusty allies appeared in public together on behalf of Free Trade views. The first time they met was when Bright, then quite a stripling, walked one day into Mr. Cobden's warehouse to solicit him to come to Rochdale to address an education meeting. He accepted the invitation; Bright himself also spoke, and Cobden was so struck with him that he sought to press him wholly into the Anti-Corn-Law cause. Bright, who married young, lost his wife shortly after marriage. He went to Leamington, where Cobden visited him, and found him bowed down by grief. "Come with me," said Cobden, "and we will never rest until we abolish the Corn Laws." Bright arose and went with him; and thus was his great sorrow turned to the nation's and the world's advantage.

The campaign of 1840 was commenced with extraordinary vigor. A numerous meeting of delegates was to be held in Manchester. The town contained no hall large enough to contain half of the *members* of the League resident in Manchester and its immediate vicinity. And the Leaguers desired to bring as many *opponents* of their views as possible within the range of their voices. Here was a difficulty. Mr. Cobden, ever ready, solved it. He happened to own nearly all the land in Saint Peter's Field, in which the Peterloo massacre had been perpetrated more than twenty years previously. Cobden offered the site; it was accepted; and the great and commodious Free Trade Hall thereon ultimately erected. Meanwhile an immense temporary pavilion was raised, by the work of a hundred men for eleven days. It was resolved to inaugurate the opening of the pavilion by a banquet. The public eagerness to be present was immense, for the Leaguers had secured a coadjutor of enormous power and value. Daniel O'Connell arrived in Manchester in time for the banquet, being met by thousands of enthusiastic admirers at the railway, and escorted by them to the pavilion. All the leading Free Trade members of Parliament and delegates from the chief towns of the empire were present. O'Connell was the hero of the evening, and delivered one of his greatest speeches. Cobden immediately followed him; but so great was his modesty, and so little idea does he as yet seem to have entertained of the leading place he was yet to take in the struggle, that he only made a short speech of ten minutes. John Bright was not even on the platform, but occupied a humble position among the mass of the auditors. Brief as was Cobden's speech, it was long enough to contain a fine demonstration of the world-wide, as well as national, aspect of the question. " We have here," said he, " gentlemen from almost every region of the globe. We have here gentlemen from Mexico, and from the United States; from Paris and St. Petersburg; from Odessa and Geneva. Indeed, I scarcely know a town within the German League which is not represented here to-night. They will unite the Baltic and the Black Sea, and cover their rivers with commerce as the rivers of England are covered. The object of the Anti-Corn-Law League is to draw together in the bonds of friendship— to unite in the bonds of amity the whole world." The leading speakers on this occasion were Dr. Bowring, Sharman Crawford, George Thompson, and Ebenezer Elliot. Mr. Milner Gibson made his first appearance, on this night, on a Free Trade platform, and made a most favorable impression. On the next night a working-men's banquet was held, five thousand men being in the hall, the fe-

male members of their families filling the galleries.
Mr. Cobden was again one of the speakers.

One of the events of 1840 was the interview
of a deputation of the Leaguers, Cobden being
one, with Lord Melbourne. Cobden expressed to
his lordship with emphasis the strong desire of
the Free Traders to have all taxes supposed to act
protectively to manufactures removed, as well as
the tax on bread. At the end of the conference,
Melbourne said he could not pledge himself to
repeal. He acknowledged the respectability of
the deputation, but had the ineffable assurance
to add that the government did not assume responsibility or initiation in the matter, but left
them to the House of Commons! One of the
deputation rejoined: "My lord, we leave you
with the consciousness of having done our duty,
and the responsibility for the future must rest
upon the government." Melbourne's easy *insou-
ciant* tone proved very valuable to the League.
It evoked instant indignation, and brought in at
once many recruits and large subscriptions.

A subsequent deputation which waited upon
Mr. Baring, the Chancellor of the Exchequer, and
Mr. Labouchere, the President of the Board of
Trade, presented one of the most extraordinary
scenes ever witnessed in a Downing-Street Office.
We prefer to present it in the words of Mr. Pren-
tice, for he was a spectator of, and a participant
in it: "Mr. J. B. Smith began the conference in

a modest and respectful, but perfectly firm manner. . . . . . Mr. John Brooks, the worthy Boroughreeve of Manchester, followed, and stated, unmoved, many instances of serious depression in the property of men of his own class; but when he came to give a detail of the distresses of the working classes, and to describe one particular family, the members of which, after a life of economy and industry, had been compelled to pawn articles of furniture and clothes, one after another, till nothing was left but bare walls and empty cupboards, his feelings completely overpowered him; convulsive sobs choked his utterance, and he was obliged to pause till he recovered from his deep emotion. The tears rolled down the cheeks of Joseph Sturge; John Benjamin Smith strove in vain to conceal his feelings; there was scarcely a tearless eye in the multitude; and the ministers looked with perfect astonishment at a scene so unusual to statesmen and courtiers. . . . . . Joseph Sturge made a powerful appeal to the ministers, placing the whole question upon the eternal principles of justice and morality, which, he said, were shamefully outraged by a tax on the food of the people. The conference, if such it could be called, where unpalatable truths were forced upon the attention of unwilling ears, was appropriately closed by some bold and really eloquent remarks from Mr. Cobden, who told the ministers that their decision would become a matter of history, and 'would stamp their character either as representatives merely of class interests, or the promoters of an enlightened commercial policy.'"

Up to this date the Anti-Corn-Law Leaguers had believed—or hoped—that some dependence might be placed in the Whig party. Many of its members had declared themselves against the Corn Laws when out of office, and it was hoped, after they had had handed to them the reins of the state, they might lend a friendly hand to those who were contesting the great landowners' monopoly. The cold responses of Lord Melbourne, Mr. Baring, and Mr. Labouchere thoroughly dissipated the last remnants of that faint hope, and the League now declared themselves formally to that effect. Immediately after the interviews which we have just chronicled, they passed a resolution, "That, dissociating ourselves from all political parties, we hereby declare that we will use every exertion to obtain the return of those members to Parliament alone who will support a repeal of the Corn Laws." The official Whigs laughed at this. "For eight or nine years they had found that the cry of 'do not embarrass the administration,' and 'keep the Tories down,' had drawn around them those who had occasionally shown a disposition to diverge into more radical courses. They thought the same cry would serve them in any emergency, and they laughed at the notion that the assertion of an 'abstract principle' would withdraw any of their usual supporters from their party allegiance." Ere many years they found their mistake.

It was now determined that the leading members of the League, as well as the paid and professional lecturers, should go forth and address meetings as itinerants. Cobden began to take his fair share of the work. And he astonished his coadjutors by the power he displayed of addressing arguments to the roughest understandings, and even disarming the objections of the most prejudiced opponents—working-men who had been directed on the wrong scent by the Tories, and their allies the Chartists. His colleagues had feared until now "that he was a little too refined for the rough work of a popular meeting."

Ladies were now enlisted in the holy and righteous propaganda. It was found that they took a deep interest in the subject which so engrossed their fathers, husbands, and brothers: one old lady of eighty said that, "in her daily prayers for bread, she also prayed for a blessing on the good work of Richard Cobden." The first of the great League tea-parties was held in the Manchester Corn Exchange, in October, 1840. Mrs. Cobden presided at one of the tables, and her husband was one of the speakers. With customary Tory courtesy, the ladies were reproached by the monopolists and their toady abettors with "indelicacy." The ladies could well despise the taunt, for these tea-meetings proved most serviceable to the cause. They required no champion; but a most redoubtable one appeared in the person of Frederic Bastiat. "If woman," said he, "does become alarmed at the dull syllogism and cold statistics, she is gifted with a marvelous sagacity, with a promptitude and certainty of appreciation, which make her detect at once on what side a serious emphasis sympathizes with the tendencies of her own heart. She has comprehended that the effort of the League is a cause of justice and of reparation toward the suffering classes; she has comprehended that almsgiving is not the only form of charity. We are ready to succor the unfortunate, say they; but that is no reason why the law should make unfortunates. We are willing to feed those who are hungry, to clothe those who are cold, but we applaud efforts which have for their object the removal of the barriers which interpose between clothing and nakedness, between subistence and starvation. . . . . In former times the ladies crowned the conqueror of the tourney. Valor, address, clemency, became popularized by the intoxicating sound of their applause. In those times of trouble and of violence, in which brutal force overrode the feeble and the defenseless, it was a good thing to encourage the union of the generosity which is found in the courage and loyalty of the knight with the rude manners of the soldier. What!

because the times are changed ; because the age is advanced ; because muscular force has given place to moral energy; because injustice and oppression borrow other forms, and strife is removed from the field of battle to the conflict of ideas, shall the mission of woman be terminated ? Shall she be always restricted to the rear of the social movement ? Shall it be forbidden to her to exercise over new customs her benignant influence, or to foster under her regard the virtues of a more elevated order which modern civilization has called into existence ?"

In 1841, the Melbourne administration, which had been during the latter part of its existence as unpopular as a government could well be, was evidently tottering to its fall. Without any premonition, and to the surprise of both parties, Lord John Russell gave notice of a motion " that the House resolve itself into a committee of the whole House, to consider of the acts relating to the trade in corn." Every body at once said that ministers were going to dissolve; that they wished a good "cry," and were bidding for the support and alliance of the League. When the disclosure was fully made, and Lord John proposed a fixed duty of eight shillings, the mind of the League was made up at once; indeed, it had been made up in anticipation should the contingency occur which now had arisen. The League at once communicated with all its auxiliary associations, urging them to redouble their efforts, for ministers were evidently feeling their way, and might, if the country showed unquestionable earnestness, concede the whole. Meeting after meeting followed in rapid succession, Cobden attending a much larger proportion than he had hitherto done, and advanced day by day in the admiration of his colleagues and the public. It was now agreed that a strong effort must be made to return him to Parliament; a sufficient proof that he had now attained the very first rank. Lord John Russell, as midsummer approached, brought forward his complete financial statement, which comprised signal steps in the direction of Free Trade, especially in the items of timber and sugar. The Leaguers willingly admitted this; but no equivalent, of however tempting a character, would they accept in lieu of the utter abolition of the Corn Laws. At one of the League meetings held this summer, Mr. Cobden, by this time, though but thirty-seven years old, enjoying an income not far short of £10,000 a year, used this strong language: "Beginning myself without one shilling besides what I derived from my own industry, I have pushed my way along, but I declare it as my firm conviction that, had I been left to commence my career at the present day, such is the state of trade, I could not have a chance of rising. Let the young men who fill our warehouses think of this, and they will see the deep interest they have in this matter." Cobden's fitting and telling speeches were by this time so popular, that if he appeared on a League platform, even if not set down in the evening's programme, or himself intending to speak, he was sure to be called for by the audience, and was obliged to address them.

Sir Robert Peel defeated ministers on a vote of confidence by a majority of one, and they determined to go to the country. At the election, which as a whole returned a Conservative majority of seventy-six—a nemesis on the Whigs which their

own once warm friends, the Radicals, did not regret—the League secured several seats. At Wal-
sall their candidate was triumphantly returned.
Bowring sat for Bolton, Cobden for Stockport.
Two Free Traders, but giving a preference to
the Whig ministers on grounds of party, were returned for Manchester : these were Mark Phillips
and Milner Gibson.

Mr. Cobden embraced the first opportunity
that presented itself of addressing the Parliament
to which he had been admitted. His maiden
speech was delivered on the 25th of August, being
the second night of the debate on the address
in answer to the queen's speech. Miss Martineau thus describes his first appearance, and the
opinions formed of it :

"When the daily papers of the 26th of August
had reached their destinations throughout the
island, there were meditative students, anxious
invalids in their sick-chambers, watchful philos-
ophers, and a host of sufferers from want, who
felt that a new era in the history of England had
opened, now that the People's Tale had at last
been told in the People's House of Parliament.
Such observers as these, and multitudes more,
asked of all who could tell them who this Richard
Cobden was, and what he was like ; and the answer was, that he was the member of a calico-
printing firm in Manchester ; that it was supposed
that he would be an opulent man if he prose-

cuted business as men of business generally do, but that he gallantly sacrificed the pursuit of his own fortune, and his partners gallantly spared him to the public, for the sake of the great cause of Corn Law Repeal—his experience, his liberal education, and his remarkable powers all indicating him as a fitting leader in the enterprise. It was added that his countenance was grave, his manner simple and earnest, his eloquence plain, ready, and forcible, of a kind eminently suited to his time and his function, and wholly new in the House of Commons. It was at once remarked that he was not treated in the House with the courtesy usually accorded to a new member, and it was perceived that he did not need such observance. However agreeable it might have been to him, he did not expect it from an assemblage proud of ' the preponderance of the landed interest' within it; and he could do without it. Some, who had least knowledge of the operative classes, and the least sympathy for them, were touched by the simplicity and manliness with which the new member received the jeers which followed his detailed statements of ' the proportion of the bread duty paid by men who must support their families on ten shillings a week.' "

We offer no excuse for making considerably more lengthened citation from Cobden's first speech in Parliament than we shall be enabled to do in the case of any of those delivered subsequently, and we strike into it at the passage referred to by Miss Martineau:

"He called the attention of the House to the working of the Bread Tax. The effect was this: it compelled the working classes to pay 40 per cent. more, that is, a higher price than they should pay if there was a free trade in corn. When honorable gentlemen spoke of 40s. as the price of foreign corn, they would make the addition 50 per cent. He did not overstate the case, and therefore he set down the bread tax as imposing an additional tax of 40 per cent. He had now to call their attention to facts contained in the Report of the Committee on the Hand-loom Weavers. It was a report got up with great care and singular talent. It gave, among other things, the amount of the earnings of a working-man's family, and that was put down at ten shillings. Looking at the metropolitan and rural districts, they found that not to be a bad estimate of the earnings of every laboring family. But let them proceed upward, and see how the same tax worked. The man who had 20s. a week still paid 2s. a week to the bread tax; that was to him 10 per cent., as an income tax. If they went farther, to the man who had 40s. a week, the income tax upon him in this way was 5 per cent. If they mounted higher, to the man who had £5 a week, or £250 a year, it was 1 per cent. income tax. Let them ascend to the nobility and the millionaires, to those who had an income of £200,000 a year. His family was the same as the poor man's, and how did the bread tax affect him? It was one half penny in every £100. [Here, we presume, there were some manifestations of derision.] He did not know whether it was the monstrous injustice of the case, or the humble individual who stated it, that excited this manifestation of feeling; but, still, he *did* state that the nobleman's family paid to this bread tax but one halfpenny in every £100 as income tax, while the effect of the tax upon the laborer's family was 20 per cent."

We have of set purpose omitted, at a recent stage of our narrative, the record of one of the most important and effective alliances which Cobden and his coadjutors effected at a date just previous to the assembling of the new Parliament, preferring to reserve its insertion in the words of Cobden in this speech: " Probably honorable gentlemen were aware that a very important meeting had been lately held at Manchester; he alluded to the meeting of ministers of religion. (A laugh.) He understood that laugh; but he should not pause in his statement of facts, but might perhaps notice it before concluding. He had seen a body of ministers of religion of all denominations—650 (and not thirty) in number— assembled from all parts of the country, at an expense of from three to four thousand pounds,

paid by their congregations. At that meeting
most important statements of facts were made
relating to the condition of the laboring classes.
He would not trouble the House by reading these
statements, but they showed that in every district of the country—and these statements rested
upon unimpeachable authority—the condition of
the great body of her majesty's laboring population had deteriorated woefully within the last ten
years, and more especially within the last three
years, and that in proportion as the price of food
increased, in the same proportion the comforts of
the working classes had diminished. One word
in respect to the manner in which his allusion to
this meeting was received. He did not come
there to vindicate the conduct of these Christian
men in having assembled in order to take this
subject into consideration. The parties who had
to judge them were their own congregations.
There were at that meeting members of the Established Church, of the Church of Rome, In-
dependents, Baptists, members of the Church of
Scotland, and of the Secession Church, Method-
ists, and, indeed, ministers of every other denom-
ination; and if he were disposed to impugn the
character of those divines, he felt he should be
casting a stigma and a reproach upon the great
body of professing Christians in this country. He
happened to be the only member of the House
present at that meeting; and he might be allow-

ed to state that, when he heard the tales of misery there described—when he heard these ministers declare that members of their congregations were kept away from places of worship during the morning service, and only crept out under cover of the darkness of night—when they described others as unfit to receive spiritual consolation because they were sunk so low in physical destitution — that the attendance at Sunday-schools was falling off—when he heard these, and such like statements—when he who believed that the Corn Laws, the provision monopoly, was at the bottom of all that was endured, heard these statements, and from such authority, he must say that he rejoiced to see gentlemen of such character come forward, and, like Nathan, when he addressed the owner of flocks and herds who had plundered the poor man of his only lamb, say unto the doer of injustice, whoever he might be, 'Thou art the man.' The people, through the ministers, had protested against the Corn Laws. Those laws had been tested by the immutable morality of Scripture. Those reverend gentlemen had prepared and signed a petition, in which they prayed the removal of those laws—laws which, they stated, violated the Scriptures, and prevented famishing men from having a portion of those fatherly bounties which were intended for all people; and he would remind honorable gentlemen that, besides these 650 ministers, there were 1500 others from whom letters had been received, offering up their prayers in the several localities to incline the will of Him who ruled princes and potentates to turn your hearts to justice and mercy. When they found so many ministers of religion, without any sectarian differences, joining heart and hand in a great cause, there could be no doubt of their earnestness. He begged to call to their minds whether these worthy men would not make very efficient ministers in this great cause? They knew what they had done in the anti-slavery question, when the religious public was roused; and what the difference was between stealing a man and making him labor, and robbing a man of the fruit of his industry, he could not perceive. The noble lord, the member for North Lancashire (Lord Stanley), knew something of the abilities of those men. The noble lord had told the House that from the moment the religious community and their pastors took up the question of slavery, from that moment the agitation must be successful. He believed this would be the case in the present instance. Englishmen had a respect for rank, for wealth, perhaps too much; they felt an attachment to the laws of their country; but there was another attribute in the minds of Englishmen—there was a permanent veneration for sacred things; and where their sympathy, and respect, and deference were enlisted in what they believed to be a sacred cause, YOU AND YOURS (said Cobden, with sudden fire, addressing the Tories) WILL VANISH LIKE CHAFF BEFORE THE WHIRLWIND!"

"Much of this speech," says Miss Martineau, "relating to the great meeting of religious ministers at Manchester, and its tone being determined accordingly, some of the laughing members of the House called Mr. Cobden a Methodist parson, and were astonished afterward to find what his abilities were in widely different directions. Some regarded him as a pledged Radical in politics, and were surprised to see him afterward verifying the assurances he gave this night—that he belonged to no party, and, as a simple Free Trader, would support either the Whigs or Sir Robert Peel, whichever of them should go farthest in repealing the restrictions on food." This political neutrality of the League was as distinctly declared by Cobden in the House as it had been on the hustings. His concluding words were: "I assure the House that the declarations I have made were not made with a party spirit. I do not call myself Whig or Tory. I am a Free Trader, and opposed to monopoly wherever I find it. And this I will conscientiously say, that though proud to acknowledge the virtues of the Whigs in stepping out from the ranks of the monopolists, and going three fourths of the way, if the right honorable baronet (Peel) and his supporters would come a step forward, I would be the first to shake hands with him, if he allowed me, and would give him a cordial support." There was something here almost prophetic of the great event of five years later.

Amendments to the address having been carried by large majorities in both Houses, ministers resigned, and that administration of Peel, which was destined to be so fruitful of beneficial consequences to the nation, was inaugurated. A short autumnal session was held, the premier reserving the statement of his financial policy until the spring. The League at once burst into still greater activity. There were more lecturers and more tracts; a splendid bazar, by which £9000 were netted, at Manchester; and another conference of Christian ministers at Edinburg. And a third convention was appointed to meet in London on the reassembling of Parliament.

Ere the autumnal session was closed, Cobden spoke in terms of the strongest denunciation of the premier's refusal to announce his financial policy—in other words, his proposals for relief to the prevailing distress—until the succeeding year. The distress was indeed terrible. "Cobden unmistakably placed the responsibility of its continuance on the proper shoulders." "In the borough of Stockport, which he represented, the distress was fearful; one out of every five houses in Stockport was untenanted, half of those occupied were not paying rent; nearly half of the manufacturers' mills were closed, and thousands of working people, who to other countries would be a valuable possession, were wandering about the street seeking employment, but unable to find it. Yet, in the face of such facts, were they to wait five months for measures of relief? God knew whether or not he should have constituents in five months. If emigration went on for the next six months as it had done for the last twelve months, he feared he should find very few of his constituents left. If, however, they were to have the discussion adjourned for six months, he begged leave to place the responsibility, and the particular consequences to the laboring population that would flow from such a course, on the shoulders of the right honorable gentlemen opposite. They had fraternized with the Chartists to some purpose during the last twelve months. A coalition had taken place between them, which he believed was now about to be dissolved; but let them beware, when going back to a people deprived of work, discontented and dissatisfied, that the cause of the delay was placed on the right shoulders. It was right that the working classes should know that they had six months of privation and suffering before them merely because certain honorable members were desirous not to miss the pleasures of shooting!"

It would be impossible for us, within the prescribed limits of our performance, to present more than the succinctest summary of the doings of Cobden and the League during the years that were yet to intervene ere their labors were crowned with complete and final success. We must be content to present a series of the more salient incidents of the agitation, preserving a due and proportionate prominence for the parliamentary appearances and the platform utterances of the subject of our biographic sketch.

At a great aggregate meeting held at Derby in November, 1842, Mr. Cobden made a most lucid exposition of the fallacies of the most loudly-uttered objections against the cause to which he had dedicated his extraordinary energies. He was addressing more especially the manufacturers of Nottinghamshire, Leicestershire, and Derbyshire, the peculiarities and conditions of whose crafts differed considerably from those of the more northern counties. The extraordinary versatility of Cobden, and his capacity of adapting the style and tone of his arguments to the circumstances, sympathies, and prejudices of his auditors, whoever they might be, from M.P.'s down to the most violent of the Chartists, was one of his most remarkable traits, and one in which no man in our century, with the sole exception of O'Connell, rivaled him. This characteristic is very manifest in the speech from which we here briefly quote: "Allow me to say that, listening to the details which you have given to-day, going back for a period of five-and-twenty years, showing a constant depression in the condition of the people, and a decline in your own immediate interests, I could not help thinking—pardon me for saying so—that the agitation against the corn and provision law should have been begun long, long ago in the Midland Counties. Why, gentlemen, you have the whole of the case in your own hands. We in Lancashire fight under a disadvantage; we are told, when we call for a repeal of the corn and provision monopoly, that our distress arises from improvement in machinery. But this does not apply to your case, for I am told that the stocking-frame has remained nearly the same as when it issued from the hands of the inventors two centuries ago; at all events, I believe that within the last five-and-twenty years no material alterations have taken place in the machine; and there are no steam-engines with tall chimneys planted here, giving motion to the power-loom instead of the stocking-frame. Then we are met in Manchester again with the cry that over-production is the cause of all the distress. But I have heard to-day that your production is declining; that the number of frames in motion is diminishing instead of increasing, especially in Leicestershire. It is, therefore, not over-production, it is not machinery, that is doing the mischief for you. But what do you hear also in Lancashire? That joint-stock

banks have produced all the distress. But here
I find that no great mischief has been produced
by joint-stock banks. You, therefore, have the
case in your own hands. The whole of the fallacies of our opponents, as applied to Manchester,
are answered in your case; and I say that, with
such a case in your hands, and with such claims
on the part of your dependents, henceforth it becomes the province of the Midland Counties to
take up the question, to lead onward in the van,
and to be the champions for the total and immediate repeal of the Corn Laws."

In the same speech Mr. Cobden thus aptly drew
the notice of his auditors to the pretense of " burdens on land," and what he frequently described
as the " Land-Tax Fraud:" " Exactly 149 years
ago, when the landed aristocracy got possession
of the throne in the person of King William, at
our glorious revolution, they got rid of all the old
tenures and services, such as the crown having the
right of wardship over every minor, the fines pay-
able on the descent of certain property from one
person to another, and a thousand other similar
incumbrances, which yielded the whole revenue
of the state; and besides which, the land had to
find soldiers and maintain them. These incumbrances were given up for a *bonâ fide* rent-charge
upon the land of four shillings in the pound; and
the land was valued and assessed 149 years ago
at £9,000,000; and upon that valuation the Land

Tax is still laid. Now, you gentlemen of the middle classes, whose windows are counted, and who have a schedule sent to you every year, in which you are required to state the number of your dogs and horses; and you who have not window and dog duty to pay, but who consume sugar, and coffee, and tea, and pay a tax for every pound you consume extra—I say to you, remember that the landowners have never had their land re-valued from 1696 to the present time."

In March of the following year, in his place in the House of Commons, Cobden pursued the same subject in more copious detail, and in an elaborate speech, bristling with irrefragable figures and facts, from which we can only afford space for a brief extract, utterly demolished the delusion that any special fiscal burdens afflicted the land: "Honorable gentlemen claimed the privilege of taxing our bread on account of their peculiar burdens in paying the highway rates and the tithes. Why, the land had borne those burdens before Corn Laws were thought of. The only peculiar state burden borne by the land was the Land Tax, and he would undertake to show that the mode of levying that tax was fraudulent and evasive—an example, in fact, of legislative partiality and injustice second only to the Corn Law itself. . . . . For a period of 150 years after the Conquest, the whole of the revenue of this country was derived from the land. During the next 150 years it yielded nineteen twentieths of the revenue. For the next century, down to the reign of Richard the Third, it was nine tenths. During the next seventy years, to the time of Mary, it fell to about three fourths. From this time to the end of the Commonwealth, land appears to have yielded half the revenue. Down to the reign of Anne it was a fourth. In the reign of George I. it was one fifth. In George the Second's reign it was one sixth. For the first thirty years of George the Third's reign, the land yielded one seventh of the revenue. From 1793 to 1816 (during the period of the Property Tax), land contributed one ninth; from which time to the present, one twenty-fifth only of the revenue has been derived directly from land. Thus the land, which anciently paid the whole of the taxation, paid now only a fraction, or one twenty-fifth, notwithstanding the immense increase which had taken place in the value of the rentals. The people had fared better under the despotic monarchs than when the powers of the state had fallen into the hands of a landed oligarchy, who first exempted themselves from taxation, and next claimed compensation by a corn law for their heavy and peculiar burdens!"

The following facts furnish a tolerably fair indication of Mr. Cobden's pluckiness—we can employ no better term—at this early, and, as some thought, hopeless period of the Anti-Corn-Law agitation. The League held one of its usual meetings at the dullest, and saddest, and most distress-

ing period of the year at Manchester. Silk Buckingham was introduced. Every one remembered
what good service he had rendered to the state
by his lectures in former years against the East
India monopoly. He addressed the meeting; so
did homely Joseph Brotherton, whose very sensible annual motions that the House of Commons
should dismiss itself and betake itself to bed at the
sensible hour of twelve every night many of our
readers will recollect. But there was a sort of
damper on the meeting. Mr. Cobden jumped up
with alacrity, and, to cheer his friends up, first
informed them that Mr. Buckingham was going to
join their gallant crew as a recruit; he was going
to become one of their lecturers. Then he said he
was for national co-operation; it must be a mere
Manchester matter no longer. The League must
print a million copies of each of their three prize
essays. In a fortnight he'd have every Manchester printing-press in full swing. They must not
any longer dispense Free Trade tracts, but condensed *libraries* on the Corn Laws. Every lecturer must have his district. And as for the monopolist papers jeering them and saying they
wouldn't raise their £50,000, why he thought they
might just as well ask for a hundred thousand at
once. They'd say this to the country—" We'll
spend the money first; we'll put ourselves in
pledge for it, and we'll trust to our bread-eating
countrymen to take us out of pawn !"

F

CHAPTER V.

PROGRESS OF THE FREE TRADE AGITATION.

AFTER the five months' gestation by the ministry which we have seen Mr. Cobden so indignantly denounce, Sir Robert Peel brought in his famous budget of 1842, with its sliding scale, its abolition, or reduction of 750 duties of greater or lesser importance, and its other well-known features.   Cobden and the League would not accept that portion of it which had reference to corn.   Delegates were at once again, to the number of six hundred, sent to London, and, to the infinite annoyance of ministers, made preparations for a session concurrently with that of Parliament, at their head-quarters in Palace Yard.   On one occasion the deputies proceeded in a body to the House of Commons.   They were flatly refused admission into the House.   They congregated round the entrance, shouting "Total repeal" and "Cheap food" as the members entered.   After giving three hearty cheers for Free Trade, they dispersed, and on their way backward met the carriage of Sir Robert Peel.   "He seemed," says an eye-witness, "at first, as if they were going to cheer him; but when he heard the angry shouts,

'No Corn Law,' 'Give bread and labor,' he lean-
ed back in his carriage grave and pale." The
question before the country was between Sir
Robert's plan of a fluctuating duty and Lord
John Russell's proposition of a fixed one. Mr.
Cobden, at an early period of a long-protracted
debate, protested against both in one of his most
vigorous and telling speeches. He dealt especially with the fallacy, whose antiquity was exactly
coeval with that of the Corn Law itself, that high
prices of corn produced a high rate of wages. He
accused the Tories of utter ignorance on the subject; and being met thereupon with a storm of
deprecatory and derisive "Oh! oh's!" he turned
to the benches whence they proceeded, and said,
"Yes! I say an ignorance upon this subject which
I never saw equaled in any body of working-men
in the north of England. (Oh, oh.) Do you
think that the fallacy of 1815, which to my astonishment I heard put forth in the House last
week, namely, that wages rise and fall with the
price of food, can prevail, after the experience of
the last three years? Have you not had bread
higher during that time than during any two
years during the last twenty years? Yes. Yet,
during these three years, the wages of labor in
every branch of industry have suffered a greater
decline than in any three years before."

One of the most important articles affected by
Peel's great and sweeping financial measure was

sugar. Manipulating it generally in the direction
of reduction, he also abated the differential duty
which had hitherto obtained against slave-grown
sugar. This caused great grief to many sincere
friends of the slave and of freedom; and among
others, stanch Free Trader though he was, to Joseph Sturge. Cobden thought otherwise. He
thought that slavery was not to be put down by
tariffs. "You and I," said he, in a letter written
some years after, but on the same subject, "do
not disagree in our abhorrence of slavery, nor do
I yield to any one in sympathy for the victims of
that sin, but we do differ as to the course which
we ought to take, *by legislation*, in this country
to put down the slave-trade." While the controversy was at its red heat, Cobden sent to Sturge
the following jocular *brochure* on this question.
It is perhaps necessary to state that the Lord
Ripon who is one of the interlocutors is Cobbet's
"Prosperity Robinson," the gentleman who was
prime minister of England for a few weeks, and
who was also President of the Board of Trade under Peel. This premised, the rest explains itself.

"A SCENE AT THE BOARD OF TRADE.

"LORD RIPON *and the* BRAZILIAN EMBASSADOR
sitting together.

"*Embassador.* Your lordship is doubtless
aware that the commercial treaty between England and Brazil is about to expire?

"*Ripon*. True; and I am happy to find myself empowered to treat with your excellency for a renewal of the commercial relations between the two countries, so admirably calculated by nature to minister to the wealth and happiness of each other.

"*Embassador*. Brazil is favored beyond almost any other country in its soil, climate, and the facilities of its internal communication. Its products are various, comprising hides, tallow, cotton, gems of a variety of kinds, sugar—

" *Ripon*. I beg your excellency's pardon for interrupting you, but how is your sugar. cultivated—by slave labor?

"*Embassador*. It is.

" *Ripon*. Oh, strike it out of the list, I beg; we can not take slave sugar; it is contrary to the religious principles of the British people to buy slave-grown sugar—*it is stolen goods*.

"*Embassador*. I bow to your nation's honorable scruples. We will then omit the sugar. Still there are other commodities remaining in which we may effect a profitable exchange, and, I hope, to the benefit of both countries.

" *Ripon*. Oh yes, there are plenty of articles of exchange which we shall still be happy to supply you with—our irons, earthenware, silks, woolens, cottons—

" *Embassador*. I beg pardon; did your lordship say cottons?

"*Ripon.* Yes; we are the largest dealers in cotton goods in the world, and we sell them so cheap that they find their way more or less into every country on the face of the earth: we supply Italy—

"*Embassador.* I pray your lordship's pardon for again interrupting you, but may I ask how is the cotton cultivated; is it not by slave labor?

"*Ripon.* Why, ahem! how is it cultivated, you say? Why, ahem!—hem!—why—

"*Embassador.* I believe I can relieve your lordship from your apparent embarrassment by answering that question. At least four fifths of the cotton imported into England is of slave cultivation.

"*Ripon.* Ahem! I believe it is so.

"*Embassador.* Then am I to understand that your people have no religious scruple against selling slave-grown produce to the Brazilians?

"*Ripon.* (Colors in his face, and moves about uneasily in his chair.)

"*Embassador.* No religious scruples against selling slave-grown cottons into every country in the world!—no religious scruples against eating slave-grown rice!—no religious scruples against making slave-grown tobacco!—no religious scruples against taking slave-grown snuff! (pointing to a gold snuff-box lying on the table.) Am I to understand that the religious scruples of the English people are confined to the article of sugar?

"*Ripon*. (Putting the snuff-box in his pocket.) I am sorry to be obliged to repeat that I can not consent to take your sugar.

"*Embassador*. (Rising from his seat.) My lord, I should be first to do homage to the sincere and consistent scruples of conscientious Christians; but while you are sending to Brazil sixty millions of yards of cotton goods in a year, I can not, in justice to my own feelings, sit quietly and listen to the plea that your nation has in reality any religious scruples upon the subject of slave-labor. Excuse me if I suggest to your lordship that other reasons may be found, especially in the monopoly which your colonial proprietors enjoy—

"*Ripon*. (Interrupting him.) I do assure your excellency that a body of religious men, the anti-slavery party, have urged these scruples upon her majesty's government. I have to-day been waited upon by Joseph Sturge, one of the most influential of that body—

"*Embassador*. Joseph Sturge! I have heard of him and his labors in the cause of humanity. He is the consistent friend of the oppressed—too consistent, I should hope, to urge upon his government, while making a treaty with the Brazils for receiving slave-grown cotton from your country, to refuse slave-grown sugar in exchange. Joseph Sturge is a believer in the New Testament, which teaches us to 'remove the beam from our own eye before we cast out the mote from our neighbor's eye.' Does not Joseph Sturge oppose the introduction into this country of cotton, tobacco, and rice?

" (The door opens, and enter Joseph Sturge, with a cotton cravat, his hat lined with calico, his coat, etc., sewn with cotton thread, and his cotton pockets well lined with slave-wrought gold and silver. The Brazilian embassador and Lord Ripon burst into laughter.)"

The cardinal principles of Free Trade, as applied to and incorporated in financial legislation, are, that taxes, where necessary, should be laid on for pure purposes of revenue alone; that in their remission, in the choice of those to be remitted, the interests of consumers are paramount and alone to be consulted; and that no tax should be levied in the supposed interest of producers—*that* for two reasons, each one being all-sufficient to bear the conclusion common to them both; first, that no protective tax does benefit the producer, and even if it did, he—representing the minority —has no right to enjoy it at the expense of the majority, namely, the consumers. These principles were admirably incorporated in the following passage, and so closely, clearly, and concisely put, that Peel himself was compelled completely to stultify himself by conceding the whole question at issue. How marvelous does it seem to us to-day that the Corn Laws disgraced our statute book, corrupted our Legislature, and nearly destroyed our people, for four years after the utterance of these words, and the admission which they elicited :

"You don't fix the price of cotton, or silk, or iron, or tin. Why don't you? But how are you to fix this price of corn? Going back some ten years, the right honorable baronet finds the average price of corn is 56*s.* 10*d.*; and therefore, says he, I propose to keep up the price of wheat from 54*s.* to 58*s.* The right honorable baronet's plan means that or nothing. I see in a useful little book, called the *Parliamentary Pocket Companion,* in which there are some nice little descriptions of ourselves—(laughter)—under the head 'Cayley,' that that gentleman is described as being the advocate of 'such a course of legislation with regard to agriculture as will keep wheat at 54*s.* a quarter—(hear, hear)—new milk and cheese at from 54*s.* to 60*s.* per cwt.; wool and butter at 1*s.* per lb. each, and other produce in proportion.' (Hear, hear, and laughter.) Now it might be very amusing to find that there are gentlemen still at large—(hear, hear, and great laughter)—who advocated the principle of the interposition of Parliament to fix the price at which such articles should be sold; but when we find a prime minister coming down to Parliament to avow such principles, it becomes any thing but amusing.

(Great cheering from the Opposition.)   I ask the right honorable baronet, and I pause for a reply, is he prepared to carry out that principle in the articles of cotton and wool?"   (Hear, hear.)

"Sir Robert Peel said it was impossible to fix the price of food by legislation."   (Loud cheers from the ministerial side.)

Mr. Cobden continued—"Then on what are we legislating?   (Counter cheers from the Opposition.)   I thank the right honorable baronet for his avowal.   Perhaps, then, he will oblige us by trying to do so.   Supposing, however, that he will make the attempt, I ask the right honorable gentleman—and I again pause for a reply—will he try to legislate so as to keep up the price of cotton, silk, and wool?   No reply!   Then we come to this conclusion, that we are *not* legislating for the universal people."   (Tremendous cheers.)

Nor did his lash fall upon Peel and the Tories alone.   The Whigs were glad enough, now that they were in opposition, to cheer and encourage Cobden in his denunciations of the landowner's monopoly.   But they stuck to their panacea of a fixed duty, and pleaded the difficulty, even if the Corn Laws were condemned to ultimate repeal, of abolishing them all at once.   Cobden saw no such difficulty; and thus, at the conclusion of his speech, showed them a very easy, and a *Gordian* way out of it.   " I once heard them [these scruples] met at a public meeting of electors in what appeared to me to be a very satisfactory manner. There was great difficulty on the platform among the Whig gentlemen who were assembled there about the repeal of the Corn Laws, and they were arguing about the danger and hardship of an immediate repeal of them. They were at length interrupted by a sturdy laboring man in a fustian coat, who called out, ' Whoi, mun, where's the trouble in taking them off? you put them on all of a ruck' (laughter and cheering); meaning that they had been put on all of a sudden."

As a specimen of the sort of arguments by which such appeals were resisted at this stage of English Parliamentary history may be cited the allegation of an M.P. whom we name not, and who spoke after Cobden, that the real motive of the Leaguers in their desire to have cheap corn was that they might have cheap flour with which to add weight and give a false appearance to their calico! Add to this, wholesale abuse of the manufacturers and the factory system, and the chief breadth of the Tory arguments is comprised and indicated. Such Protectionist " hits" were received with deafening plaudits; but we find in Hansard that when Mr. Miles, a Protectionist, said that Charles Buller had made an appeal to the " appetites as well as the passions of the people," this reference to the horrid starvation then prevailing was received with " loud laughter."

Similar "merry descants on a nation's woe" greeted Dr. Bowring's reference to any thing so miserably vulgar as the reduction in the wages of shoemakers and tailors. When he said women were crying for work, there was more "laughter;" they were making trowsers for sixpence a pair — more "loud laughter;" thousands were hungry and naked—the founts of laughter proved as prodigal as before; and "peals of loud laughter" greeted the inquiry, What was to become of the women of Manchester?

Meanwhile the League Convention continued to sit simultaneously with Parliament. Among others of its occupations, it sent deputations to wait on all the leading ministers, represent to them the true condition of the country, and impress upon them the tremendous responsibility they were incurring. But their representations were fruitless. In Parliament, Cobden, Brotherton, Villiers, Milner Gibson, and others, worked hard to get an inquiry—using every legitimate form of the House for that end. Peel bitterly reproached them with maliciously opposing the progress of public business. This brought Cobden on his legs. He retorted: "The public business referred to was the voting of the militia estimates, to put down, he supposed, the starving people. He believed they might be better employed in finding them food. If a person had the malice of a fiend, he would rejoice at the mode in which they were proceeding. The New Poor Law would not save their estates. Their present policy would create an amount of poverty that would break through stone walls. The people were now lying by the sides of hedges and walls, but when the winter came where would they go? If they were driven from the ditch-sides by the terrors of the bastiles, they would become banditti, or they must be put into the work-house. Would the right honorable baronet resist the appeals which had been made to him, or would he rather cherish the true interests of the country, and not allow himself to be dragged down by a section of the aristocracy? He must take sides, and that instantly; and should he, by doing so, displease his political supporters, there was an answer ready for them. He might say he found the country in distress, and he gave it prosperity; that he found the people starving, and he gave them food; that he found the large capitalists of the country paralyzed, and he made them prosperous." This is as nearly as could be what Peel *did* say four years later. How much human misery would have been saved if he had made the discovery when this appeal, at once to his sense and his sympathy, was made to him!

The Leaguers now resolved to turn their batteries upon the agricultural districts. The tactics of their opponents had changed, and theirs must be conformably adapted. The chief grounds held

by the Tories at this stage of the struggle were
that the movement was simply a manufacturers'
one; that its success would be as prejudicial to
the interests of the laborers, both in town and
country, as it would be beneficial to the millown-
ers; and they endeavored to damage the cause
by blackening the characters of the leaders of the
League. We are telling the story of Mr. Cobden's life as far as possible in his own words.
The greater proportion of our extracts from his
speeches are made, not with the purpose of repro-
ducing characteristic specimens of his eloquence
—a few judiciously selected passages would suffice for that—but that his public life, its motives
and actuating end, its circumstances, sorrows, and
solaces, may be moulded as nearly as possible into
an autobiographic form. It is with that view
that we make the following quotation from an autumnal speech of Mr. Cobden in this year, merely premising that thousands of the Northern operatives had "turned out" in the agony of their
desperation from their employments, asserting
that they would not return to them until their
grievances were righted:

"Now, gentlemen, I would venture to say, and
if nothing else that fell from me should go forth
to the public, I hope that this at least will do
so—I will venture to say, in the name of the
Council of the Anti-Corn-Law League, that not
only did not the members of that body know or

dream of any thing of the kind such as has now taken place—I mean the turn-out for wages—not only did they not know, concoct, wish for, or contemplate such things, but I believe the very last thing which the body of our subscribers would have wished for or desired is the suspension of their business, and the confusion which has taken place in this district. (Loud applause.) . . . . Why are these accusations made? It is with the desperate hope that they will inflict a moral taint upon the Anti-Corn-Law League. They can not oppose our principles, for their own political chief has given up the whole question, and has avowed himself to be with us in principle; they can not therefore denounce our principles; and from the moment that the prime minister declared himself a Free Trader—from the moment he said it was not only best to buy in the cheapest markets where others took goods from us, but that it was best to do so whether reciprocity existed or not (laughter and cheers) —from the moment he went that ' whole hog' in Free Trade, their mouths were closed; but still they had their dirty work to do; they must say something, and what so natural and so politic as that these miserable tools of a beaten and vanquished party should commence immediately to attack the Anti-Corn-Law League? Their only hope, their only chance now is in impairing our moral influence with the country. That is the game. . . . . We have been lately charged with being in collusion with the Chartist party. Now the parties who are charging this are laboring under the disadvantage of having themselves been working for the last three years to excite the Chartist party against us, and by means not over-creditable, as we shall by-and-by, perhaps, have the opportunity of demonstrating to the world. I will not say a word upon that at present; but, by means which may meet the light, they have succeeded in deluding a considerable portion of the working classes upon the subject of the Corn Laws. And I have no objection in admitting here, as I have admitted frankly before, that these artifices and manœuvres have, to a considerable extent, compelled us to make our agitation a middle-class agitation. I don't deny that the working classes generally have attended our lectures and signed our petitions; but I will admit that, so far as the fervor and efficiency of our agitation has gone, it has eminently been a middle-class agitation. . . . . . Let the League go on in their own course, agitating—agitating—agitating incessantly for the repeal of the Corn Laws. Gentlemen, you are strong in the country—you are stronger than you think in London. The middle classes in London are almost to a man for the repeal of the Corn Laws. You are stronger than you think in the south of England; you have strength in the rural boroughs that you are not aware of; and I will tell you now what I did not venture to say on a former occasion—that I don't think Manchester will carry the repeal of the Corn Laws, but that we shall carry it by making it a national question."

While disclaiming all party connections, Cobden invited the co-operation of all, appealing especially to the Chartists for co-operation—not *as* Chartists, but as working men. In the same speech, he said, "I believe that the working classes here generally are of opinion that the intrusion of the Chartist question has not been of any service to them in the question about wages. I believe they are quite disposed to discuss and settle this question apart from party politics. Then what will enable the master to give better wages? By getting a better price for his goods. And how is he to get a better price for his goods? By extending the markets. How can he sell more goods, and thus give more employment to labor, except he can get an enlarged market, and thus meet the wants of the increasing population of the country? There is no other way. Our business is not to alter constitutions; we don't seek for chartism, whiggism, radicalism, or republicanism—we simply ask for an enlarged market to enable the capitalist to extend the sale of his goods, and thereby to increase the demand for labor and augment the rate of wages. This is a time, gentlemen, when I hope both masters and men will meet and discuss this subject apart from party politics. The time is peculiarly favorable for this, and, I think, notwithstanding the lamentable circumstances, the state of the public mind in this country, both with masters and men, will settle down into a more rational disposition to view this question apart from passion or prejudice than ever it did before, for I do think, gentlemen, that the present disturbances will leave less of the traces of prejudice or resentment in the minds of the middle classes in this part of the country than any former tumults ever did before."

Mr. Cobden's policy was accepted, and embodied by the League. Its aim now was more than ever national. The towns being mostly secured, the object now was to gain over the country; the great mass of the urban middle class being Free Traders, propagandism must be mainly directed to the grades below them, and to the hereditary possessors of wealth and rank, their social superiors. The Tories had taunted the Leaguers with a sordid regard to their own interests, and with a selfish desire to sacrifice the peasantry to their own ends. It became highly desirable to let it be known what was the real condition of this peasantry, under the " favoring and benignant" Corn Laws. The League sent out agents to all the southern and purely agricultural counties, and took care to give proper publicity to their reports.

These were a different class of men from their lecturers. The two employments required different talents. The country-investigating agents were business-like, sharp, observing men. Their inquiry was indeed scrutinizing. You might almost believe, on consulting the reports of their investigations published by these persons, that they had inspected every field, hedge, homestead, and ditch. The general gist of their reports was a revelation of " bad tillage, and every kind of waste, overweening rents, uncertain profits, and wages reduced below the point of possible maintenance." On the estate of one nobleman, the laborers who had furnished the League agents with information, and had admitted them into their cottages to see the holes in the roofs, and the wet, soddened floors, were punished by being set to work on the roads. The moment this was discovered, the League announced that in no future case would information be sought from the laborers—the especial sufferers from Corn Laws and Protection; and they rigorously kept their word. Cobden himself went through the southern counties in the recess, holding meetings on market-days, and maintaining his ground against all comers.

At first the Protectionists made an oratorical stand against him. They brought out their loudest speakers; their speeches were elaborately prepared; the resolutions they moved and seconded carefully considered, and couched in terms as dexterous as they could devise. But it was not long ere, discovering that Cobden invariably tore their so-called arguments to ribbons, and evoked the contemptuous ridicule of their own farmer-clients, who were predisposed against him at the outset, at their sophistications, they altogether changed their tactics. The plan then was to cry Cobden down, to endeavor to drown his shrill and far-reaching voice. And then, when that failed, the procedure was to seize the wagons and drag Cobden and his associates down.

The eyes of the farmers then began to be opened. They rapidly began to join the League. Some of them were even bold enough to come out as speakers for the League. They began to see the truth which Cobden always took care to tell them—that their interests were any thing but identical with those of the men who received their rents. They saw, with clear and emancipated eyes, that they were the true "agricultural interest," and that Cobden and the League, and not the squires and the Tories, were the real "farmers' friends." Cobden told them—and, more than that, he convinced them—that landowners were just as much agriculturists as shipowners were sailors. How much Cobden did thus (like his own almost namesake, Cobbet, before him) for the cause of popular education in the best and highest sense, among the laborers and the farmers, who were not much better informed at the start than the hedgers and plowmen they employed, as well as for their physical well-being and enjoyment, it is impossible to overestimate. About leases, tenures, draining, fencing, and improved farming generally, much also was said. Cobden began to rank, and rightly so, among the rustics, not only as a farmer's friend, but as a practical farmer. And this was a great point gained. One sample of Mr. Cobden's rural meetings will do as well as another. One Saturday in June, in this year, he and his friend, Mr. Moore, visited Rye, which is in Sussex. When they got into the sleepy old town, which has been lifted up out of the sea, they found it stuck all over with placards warning the people not to be bamboozled by the idea that this Cobden was a Sussex man; for although the son of a Sussex farmer, of course he had his own interests to serve about Corn Laws, for he was a Manchester manufacturer. However, a great many of the farmers attended, Cobden having, of course, as usual, chosen market-day; and they had to adjourn from the Town Hall to the Cattle Market. Cobden gave an address, and though there was a very hostile feeling against him at first, ere he had gone far, the *Brighton Herald* of the date says, "we do not believe that there was a man present who was not convinced in his own conscience." Mr. Moore followed, and then up jumped a Major

Curteis, who said he went two thirds of the way with these gentlemen; *but* he lived where the land wasn't good, and farmers were as badly off as the laborers (a great concession this to Cobden, to which he at once responded by crying "Granted!"), and if they were repealed immediately, two out of three in his parish would have to leave their farms all at once. And he should like to know if two thirds of the tenant-farmers had to leave, how many of the laborers would be thrown out of work? Here an interlocutor, not farther dignified in the report than by the vague title of "A Voice," interrupted with, "If these tenant-farmers and laborers are in such a distressed condition, does it not arise from the enormous rents they pay?" To which the major, who, we presume, was a landlord, made the (to him) very unsatisfactory reply, that many of them paid no rents at all. He couldn't agree with Mr. Cobden that there were no exclusive burdens on the land. He thought otherwise. He'd go for repeal to-morrow, if he thought it would not throw two thirds of his neighbors into immediate distress.

Then up stood an M.P. of the same name, but not nearly so disposed to concede his point. Curteis, M.P., said he stood boldly there to contest the ground with Mr. Cobden. The point (this civilian, it will be seen, was vastly more ferocious than his namesake, and, we suppose, relative)— the point was not whether we were going to have a sliding scale or a fixed duty, but whether there was to be protection to the English farmer. Mr. Cobden said before he could attend to this gentleman, he thought another one to the right had thrown out something like a challenge about a motion to be made. He wasn't himself generally anxious about a motion. He just liked to throw out a few facts and leave them. The "gentleman to the right" didn't appear. "Well," said Cobden, "I'll claim my right as a Sussex man, and I'll propose a motion." Then he went through *Major* Curteis's " exclusive burdens on the land." " Where were they ?" said he. " Tithes belonged to the Church, never at all to the landlords; therefore *they* couldn't be a burden. Other classes as well as landlords were subject to poor rates and county rates. As for the land-tax, the less they said about that the better for themselves." Then he wound up with a motion for unconditional repeal. The major moved an amendment that " a fixed duty is desirable for the present." A division was taken, and the original motion (Cobden's) carried almost unanimously—this by an audience that at first was hostile to him.

At once the results of this tour, and the nature of the arguments used by Cobden to the farmers, will appear in these concluding sentences of a speech delivered in the House of Commons after the resumption of its session. It was on a motion for " a select committee to inquire into the effects of protective duties on imports upon the interests of the tenant farmers and farm laborers of this country." He thus concluded: "We may make a great advance if we get this committee; you may have the majority of its members Protectionists if you will. I am quite willing that such should be the arrangement. I know it is understood—at least there is a sort of etiquette —that the mover for a committee should, in the event of its being granted, preside over it as chairman. I waive all pretensions of the sort; I give up all claims; I only ask to be present as an individual member. What objections there can be to the committee I can not understand. Are you afraid that to grant it will increase agitation? I ask the honorable baronet, the member for Essex (Sir J. Tyrell), whether he thinks the agitation is going down in his part of the country? I rather think there is a good deal of agitation going on there now. Do you really think that the appointment of a dozen gentlemen, to sit in a quiet room up stairs and hear evidence, will add to the excitement out of doors? Why, by granting my committee, you will be withdrawing me from the agitation for one. But I tell you that you will raise excitement still higher than it is if you allow me to go down to your constituents — your vote against the committee in my hand—and allow me to say to them, 'I only asked for inquiry; I offered the landlords a majority of their own party; I offered them to go into committee, not as a chairman, but as an individual member; I offered them all possible advantages, and yet they would not, they dared not, grant a committee of inquiry into your condition.' I repeat to you, I desire no advantages. Let us have the committee. Let us set to work, attempting to elicit sound information, and to benefit our common country. I believe that much good may be done by adopting the course which I propose. I tell you that your boasted system is not protection, but destruction to agriculture. Let us see if we can not counteract some of the foolishness—I will not call it by a harsher name —of the doings of those who, under the pretense of protecting native industry, are inciting the farmer not to depend upon his own energy, and skill, and capital, but to come here and look for the protection of an Act of Parliament. Let us have a committee, and see if we can not elicit facts which may counteract the folly of those who are persuading the farmer to prefer Acts of Parliament to draining and subsoiling, and to be looking to the laws of this House when he should be studying the laws of Nature. I can not imagine any thing more demoralizing—yes, that is the word—more demoralizing than for you to tell the farmers that they can not compete with foreigners. You bring long rows of figures of delusive accounts, showing that the cultivation of

an acre of wheat costs £6 or £8 per year. You
put every impediment in the way of the farmers
trying to do what they ought to do. And can
you think that that is the way to make people
succeed ? How should we manufacturers get
on if, when we got as a pattern a specimen of
the productions of the rival manufacturers, we
brought all our people together and said, 'It is
quite clear that we can not compete with this
foreigner; it is quite useless our attempting to
compete with Germany or America; why, we
can not produce goods at the price at which they
do.' But how do we act in reality? We call
our men together, and say, 'So-and-so is producing goods at such a price; but we are Englishmen, and what America or Germany can do, we
can do also.'

"I repeat that the opposite system, which you
go upon, is demoralizing the farmers. Nor have
you any right to call out, with the noble lord the
member for North Lancashire—you have no right
to go down occasionally to your constituents, and
tell the farmers, 'You must not plod on as your
grandfathers did before you; you must not put
your hands behind your backs, and drag one foot
after the other in the old-fashioned style of going
to work.' I say that you have no right to hold
such language to the farmer. What makes them
plod on like their grandfathers? Who makes
them put their hands behind their backs? Why,

the men who go to Lancashire and talk of the danger of the pouring in of foreign corn from a certain province in Russia, which shall be nameless; the men who tell the farmers to look to this House for protective acts instead of their own energies—instead of to those capabilities which, were they properly brought out, would make the English farmer equal to — perhaps superior to — any in the world."

And Cobden claimed a special and authoritative right to speak on this matter, saying, " Sir, I have as good a right as any honorable gentleman in this House to identify myself with the order of farmers. I am a farmer's son. The honorable member for Sussex has been speaking to you as the farmer's friend. I am the son of a Sussex farmer; my ancestors were all yeomen of the class who have been suffering under this system; my family suffered under it, and I have, therefore, as good, or a better right, than any of you, to stand up as the farmer's friend, and to represent his wrongs in this House."

Cobden, if he had not had the thorough whip-hand of his opponents in respect of knowledge of the subjects he talked about, would have been an arrogant man. Hundreds of sayings which fell from his lips—and nowhere so frequently as in the House of Commons—if they had proceeded from an ignorant man, would have indicated the veriest and most insolent arrogance. But it is no arrogance, when you stand opposite to an ignoramus, and especially if *his* ignorance is *your* physical superior, and drives you, *nolens volens*, in its team, to denounce the ignorance and cast personal ridicule or wrath upon its human receptacle. This misanthropy—if indeed you can so call it — is begotten of philanthropy. Cobden more than once told the squirearchy not only that they were absolutely more ignorant of the prime principles of political economy than any audience of artisans he ever addressed, but that their heads were actually (he believed) so constructed that politico-economic knowledge could not get into their crania. Similarly, on one occasion, in a debate on the Game Laws, in reply to Colonel Sibthorpe, Mr. Newdegate, and others (a debate, by the way, in which Mr. Bright made his first great Parliamentary speech), Cobden talked to the class who starve peasants and fatten pheasants after this mode: He told them that country gentlemen knew infinitely less about the feelings, circumstances, and grievances of farmers than himself "and the other members of the much-maligned Anti-Corn-Law League." He said that tenant-farmers complained of nothing so much over their firesides, and when released from the surveillance of the squires and the terrorism of the gamekeepers and watchers, as the Game Laws. Here, as might have been imagined, there was one of those storms of " Oh, oh!" which only

the lusty lungs of well-fed Tories can emit. It
may be a matter of doubt whether this vocal pro-
ficiency arises from the habit of tally-hoing or of
hip-hip-hurrahing True Blue toasts. "Let the
' oh, ohs,'" quickly and angrily rejoined Cobden,
"go forth to the country, and the people will say
that the landlords know less of the country than
I do. Nay, more, I say that I have a larger correspondence with farmers, have shaken hands
with more, and talked with ten times more tenant-farmers than any other gentleman in this
House." And then, a little farther on in the
course of this pungent speech—which was also a
condensed one, for it occupied only a few minutes in the delivery—he stated the simple, bold,
undeniable, but most pregnant fact, that the enjoyment of the 60,000 persons who took out game
licenses cost the country, besides all the destruction of good human food, 4500 annual convictions
and forty transportations. Or, as he tersely put
the fact in another way, for every fifteen persons
that went shooting, one was convicted.

Some may say, "How could a man who spoke
on certain occasions in the manner that has been
represented in more than one citation in this
chapter, be described, as he constantly was by
all his friends, as a peculiarly mild, gentle, and
affectionate man? We shall save ourselves and
such of our readers equal trouble if we remind
them that the Apostle John was also a Son of

Thunder. It is the deepest and tenderest hearts that are so affected. But the motive-spring is love for the wronged, not hate of the wrong-doer.

Still the farmers joined the League. At a meeting at Manchester in November, 1843, Mr. Cobden stated, "The Council of the League had, a short time since, advertised for prize essays showing the injurious operation of the Corn Laws upon farmers and farm laborers. By the first of this month (the time limited) they received a large number. Three had been selected from that number, and, having had the opportunity of perusing them, he must say that he anticipated the greatest results from their publication. One of them was written by a tenant farmer in Scotland, paying £1500 a year rent, and he said, 'I have laid out a large sum of money, which I expect to be reimbursed for before the expiration of my lease, and yet I should be delighted to see the Corn Laws abolished before the next session of Parliament.'" A few days before, Mr. Cobden said: "An elderly person called upon me on Tuesday, having the appearance of a country gentleman, and he put this paper in my hand, accompanied by a bank-note: 'A landowner, possessed of several farms, subscribes £100 to the League fund. It is a money question, and the money speaks for itself. The subscription will be repeated, if requisite.' I never saw the gentleman before, and probably will never see him again. He did not wait for conversation ; and I could get nothing more from him than, ' It is a money question, it is a money question, and the money speaks for itself.' "

And still more accessions from the land were coming over: the Earls of Radnor and Ducie were Leaguers and subscribers to the funds; the Duke of Bedford and Earl Spencer were also with them ; and among the untitled landlords, Sharman Crawford, Gore Langton, Villiers Stuart, and Grantley Berkeley.

Perhaps the best proof of the extraordinary ferment and excitement of feeling which the Corn Law agitation produced in England is the incident we are now about to relate. It is necessary to premise that, in the January of 1843, Mr. Drummond, Sir Robert Peel's private secretary, was shot dead in the street by a lunatic, who mistook him for the premier. Peel was deeply wounded at this, for Mr. Drummond was not only his secretary, but his friend ; and he was ill and harassed with manifold anxieties. Two hours past midnight of the 17th of February, he got up and said, " Sir, the honorable gentleman (Mr. Cobden) has stated here very emphatically, what he has more than once stated at the Conferences of the Anti-Corn-Law League, that he holds me individually—[great excitement]—*individually* responsible for the distress and suffering of the country—that he holds me personally responsible; but, be the consequences of these insinuations what they may, never will I be influenced by menaces, either in this House or out of this House, to adopt a course which I consider—" [The rest of the sentence was lost in shouts from various parts of the House.]

Mr. Cobden rose and said: "I did not say that I held the right honorable gentleman responsible —[shouts of 'Yes, yes; you did, you did.' Cries of 'Order' and 'Chair.' Sir Robert Peel: 'You did.'] I have said that I hold the right honorable gentleman responsible by virtue of his office —['No, no;' much confusion]—as the whole context of what I said was sufficient to explain— ['No, no,' from the ministerial benches.]"

Sir Robert Peel rose and repeated his assertion that Cobden had "twice repeated that he held him individually responsible." At a later period of the debate, Cobden, again essaying an explanation, was hooted down. Probably a more extraordinary transaction never occurred on the floor of the House of Commons. Miss Martineau says of it, "The Anti-Corn Law League had not yet had time to win the respect and command the deference which it was soon to enjoy; but it was known to be organized and led by men of station, character, and substance — men of enlarged education, and of that virtuous and decorous conduct which distinguishes the middle class of England. Yet it was believed—believed by men of education, by men in Parliament, by men in attendance on the government—that the Anti-Corn-Law League sanctioned assassination, and did not object to carry its aims by means of it. This is, perhaps, the strongest manifestation of the tribulation of the time." It is just to the memory of Peel to insert one or two sentences uttered by him about three years later, in one of the debates on the total repeal of the Corn Laws in 1846: "The honorable member thought fit to recall to the recollection of the House something which took place about three years since, in the course of a heated debate, when I put an erroneous construction on some expressions used by the honorable member for Stockport. An explanation was given of the meaning of those expressions by that honorable member; and my intention at the time, after that explanation, was to have relieved the honorable member for Stockport, in the most distinct manner, of the imputation which I had put upon him. If any one who was present at that debate had stated to me that my reparation was not so complete, and the avowal of my error not so unequivocal as it ought to have been, I should at once have repeated it more plainly and distinctly. It was my intention to have made the fullest explanation: that my intention must have been so, will indeed appear so on reference to my speech. I am sorry,

II

certainly, that the honorable member for Shrewsbury has thought fit to revive the subject, or, at least, I should have been so if his reference to it had not given me an opportunity of fully and unequivocally withdrawing an imputation on the honorable member for Stockport, which was thrown out in the heat of debate under an erroneous impression of his meaning."

MIDHURST, SUSSEX.

CHAPTER VI.

THE VICTORY OF THE LEAGUE.

AFTER the division on Mr. Villiers's motion in 1843, the *Times* thus commented on the debate: "Mr. Cobden's speech was clever and pointed. It was creditable to his talents, as evincing an aptitude of mind and an ability to adapt his style to the air of the place and the tastes of his audience; but we do not think it was equally creditable to his judgment. A stronger impression might have been made had he abstained from personality and *persiflage*. Still, allowance must be made for a man who had to repeat a tale for the nine hundred and ninety-ninth time, and who, therefore, was compelled to adapt it to the palate of his hearers. . . . But the debate is over; the question is settled; for how long? How many even of the majority are satisfied of the working of the sliding-scale? How many of the minority would be gratified by an utter and immediate abolition of *all* corn duties?" The testimony of the *Morning Post* to the growing might of Cobden and his principles was still more significant: "Melancholy was the exhibition in the House of Commons on Monday night. Mr. Cobden was the hero of the night. Toward the close of the debate, he rose in his place, and hurled at the heads of the parliamentary landowners of England those calumnies and taunts which constitute the staple of his addresses to farmers. The taunts were not retorted. The calumnies were not repelled. No; the parliamentary representatives of the industrial interests of the British empire quailed before the founder and leader of the Anti-Corn-Law League. They winced under his sarcasms. They listened in speechless terror to his denunciations. No man among them dared to grapple with the arch-enemy of English industry. No man among them attempted to refute the miserable fallacies of which Mr. Cobden's speech was made up. . . . . Melancholy was it to witness, on Monday, the landowners of England, the representatives by blood of the Northern chivalry, the representatives by election of the industrial interests of the empire, shrinking under the blows aimed at them by a Manchester money-grubber — by a man whose importance is derived from the action of a system, destructive in its nature of all the wholesome influences that connect together the various orders of society. Well, the cycle approaches its completion; the wheel has nearly effected its revolution; and the foul and pestilential principles which, by their action, began forty years ago to consign to beggary hundreds of thousands of harmless and ingenious hand-loom weavers seem destined, if not speedily resisted, to sweep away all the barriers that still remain to shelter productive industry from the encroachment of those classes of men to whom the abasement of industry is the source of increased power and influence." We present this piece of "fine writing," because one can precisely measure, by the virulence of its spleen, the amount of power in the state which Richard Cobden and his principles had by this time attained.

As a positive and altogether more valuable indication of the spread of Free Trade principles, and of the (perhaps unexpected) support they were receiving in non-political quarters, may be given these characteristic sentences from Carlyle's "Past and Present," which was published about this time: "Oh, my Conservative friends, who still specially name, and struggle to approve yourselves 'Conservative,' would to heaven I could persuade you of this world-old fact, than which fate is not surer, that Truth and Justice alone are capable of being 'conserved' and preserved! The thing which is unjust, which is not according to God's law, will you, on a God's universe, try to conserve that? It is old, say you? Yes, and the hotter haste ought *you*, of all others, to be in to let it grow no older! If but the faintest whisper in your hearts intimate to you that it is not fair, hasten, for the sake of Conservatism itself, to probe it vigorously, to cast it forth at once and forever, if guilty. How will or can you preserve *it?* The thing is not fair. Impossible, a thousand fold, is marked on that. . . . . If I were the Conservative party of England (which is another bold figure of speech), I would not for a hundred thousand pounds an hour allow those Corn Laws to continue. All Potosi and Golconda put together would not purchase my assent to them. Do you count what treasures of bitter indignation they are laying up for you in every just English heart? Do you know what questions, not as Corn-prices and sliding-scales alone, they are forcing every reflective Englishman to ask himself? Questions insoluble or hitherto unsolved; deeper than any of our logic-plummets hitherto will sound; questions deep enough—which it were better we did not name, even in thought. You are forcing us to think of them. The utterance of them is begun; and where will it be ended, think you? When now millions of one's brother men sit in workhouses, and five millions, as is insolently said, ' rejoice in potatoes,' there are various things that must be begun, let them end where they can."

While the agitation went on in the rural districts, special new batteries were directed upon London. The extraordinary and novel step was adopted of hiring the great national theatres, in Covent Garden and Drury Lane, for the purpose of Free Trade demonstrations. These meetings were held on every successive Wednesday. They produced an immense sensation. They form to this day a marked and signal epoch in the memory of every Londoner old enough to have been an adult twenty years ago. They were sneered at as clap-trap; but it was proved that they were really effective, and dangerous to monopoly, when, shortly after their commencement, a thorough Free Trader, Mr. Pattison, was elected for the city of London, and Mr. Jones Loyd, the great banker, sent in his uncompromising adhesion to the League. Mr. Prentice, who was present, thus describes Mr. Cobden's first appearance at Drury Lane:

"Richard Cobden came last, not least, and had a reception which justified what I had heard said before, that he was the most popular man in London. I acknowledge that I was somewhat disappointed. I had heard him speak, over and over again, with more effect. I was jealous of his reputation, and grudged that he should utter one sentence without evident effect. But from him I turned to the audience, and soon perceived that they had formed a just appreciation of the man. There was not that strained attention which was seen when Mr. Fox and Mr. Gisborne addressed them, and when every one seemed prepared for a burst of enthusiasm or a burst of laughter; but there was the quiet listening si-

lence, expective, not of excitement, but of sound
instruction — the manifestly-expressed faith that
there was something well worth hearing and
well worth waiting for. And, on reflection, I
thought the more of the intelligence of the audience for this — the more of the rapidly matur-
ing public opinion of London. It seemed to say,
'Here is a man who does not strain after effect
—does not divest an argument of one thread of
sequence for effect — and is content to rest an
argument on its own intrinsic value, without artificial adornment.' And in this faith of his hearers Cobden has his strength. He gets out all he
has to say, and all he means to say. He convinces as he goes along, and with a simplicity
and plainness which seem to render conviction
irresistible. And thus are his hearers prepared
for those occasional bursts of fervor which no
man with Cobden's ideality and earnestness can
keep pent up in his own bosom. His denunciation of the wickedness of transporting the best
part of our population to find that food which
their labor would bring to them but for selfish
laws was given with all the power of a righteous
indignation, and his affecting picture of emi-
grants leaving their native land was in the finest
tone of sympathy for the sufferings of his fellow-creatures. On the one occasion and the
other, the loudly-expressed indignation and the
starting tear convinced me that the great and

brilliant audience was moved by a strong sense of justice and a deeply-felt benevolence."

The *Times* said of these theatre meetings: " A new power has arisen in the state, and maids and matrons flock to theatres as though it was but a ' new translation from the French.' "

In January, 1845, the League published certain statistics of its doings for the preceding two years. In that time it had held a hundred and fifty meetings in parliamentary boroughs, and fifty in other places ; fifteen thousand copies of the *League* newspaper—a most potent agent in the agitation —had been published weekly; more than two millions of tracts had been distributed ; and in one year thirty thousand letters had been received, and three hundred thousand dispatched. In May, 1845, a new agency, designed partly for the propagandism of the principles of the League, and partly for the augmentation of its funds, was called into play. Covent Garden Theatre was fitted up with the finest taste for a colossal Free Trade bazar. It was transformed into a fine Gothic hall, and crowded with articles of elegance or utility. Four hundred ladies acted as saleswomen. Each contributing town had its stall, with its name, and in some cases its arms, painted above. The bazar was open during the month of May ; a hundred and twenty-five thousand persons entered it, and it yielded the handsome sum of £25,000 to the funds of the League. Douglas

Jerrold said of the bazar in his "Magazine:" "A 'bazar'—'tis a trite word for a commonplace thing—often an idle mart for children's trumpery —for foolish goods brought forth of laborers' idleness. But an idea can ennoble any thing. Nobility, in its true sense, is an idea ; and how grand is the idea which ennobles *our* bazar— which, even apart from its claims as an industrial exposition, makes it a great and holy thing! 'Free Trade!' These words form a spell by which the world will yet be governed. They are the spirit of a dawning creed—a creed which already has found altars and temples worthy of its truth. The Anti-Corn-Law League Bazar has raised thoughts in the national mind which will not soon die. As a spectacle it was magnificent in the extreme, but not more grand materially than it was morally. The crowd who saw it thought as well as gazed. It was not a mere huge shop for selling wares, but a great school for propagating an idea. And the pupils were not Londoners alone. From every part of the land monster trains hurried up their visitors. From the tracts where tall chimneys stand like forests —from the districts where the plow, not the engine, labors—where the farm-steading takes the place of the factory — where the 'mill' means, not that weaving yarn, but that grinding corn— from town and country, shipping port and inland city, steam has whirled its tens of thousands to

one common centre, to see a great demonstration, to take a great lesson, and then to narrate
and teach what they have beheld and learned to
others."

This monster bazar caused a sensation in London only exceeded by the greater impression
made by the Great Exhibition of six years later.
The papers teemed with descriptions of it, and
these not only the dailies and weeklies, but the
magazines and journals dedicated to special and
professional objects. It is most amusing at this
time to observe, in those reports of its proceedings and contents which appeared in the Conservative prints, a sort of appalled wonderment
at the unexpected magnitude of the undertaking.
We are told how, notwithstanding the high price
of admission, and the tempestuousness of the
weather at its opening, it was nevertheless cram-
med to overflowing. We read of the admirable
arrangements to prevent confusion; the grand
staircase, fitted up with tapestry, carpets, and
shawls, so as to resemble an enormous draper's
shop; a magnificent mirror, " such as giants only
should survey themselves in ;" colossal boxes of
coal and iron, the latter in all stages of workman-
ship, from the crude ore to the finest and most
flexible steel; apparatus in operation weaving
soft and beautiful fabrics of glass thread; and,
finally, when the central Gothic hall is reached,
the reporter ceases to depict details, and talks

of coming suddenly upon " a scene so novel and romantic, so incongruous and grotesque, that for a moment we could fancy ourselves transported to the East, and about to deal with Turks and Mussulmans."

Our reporter finds solace in the refreshment-room, and his attention is divided between his consumption of the excellent creams and ices there vended, and the contemplation of " a huge plum-cake—a cake, the idea of which could, we think, have occurred in a dream only to some imaginative school-boy—so vast in its expanse, so ponderous its size, so rich its ingredients, so delicious its fragrance."   He thus proceeds—and we continue the extract chiefly for the sake of its latter sentences, which indicate how various were the methods, and how fertile the devices employed by Cobden and the League in their propaganda : " It (the cake) is a Bury Simnel, and measures, we should think, some five feet in diameter, weighs 280 lbs., and bears upon its broad surface a sheet of iced sugar so large as to have inscribed upon it nearly all the maxims which embody the religion of the League, and so sweet and richly ornamented as to almost induce the visitor to swallow them.   We hear that it is to be cut up and distributed on the last day of the Exhibition ; but let the League beware how they previously admit a school to their bazar, for to resist the continued temptation of this cake and its Free

Trade inscriptions is, we think, beyond the possibility of school-boy nature. In this room is also the 'post-office,' an ingenious device for (among other purposes) raising money, and disseminating Free Trade doctrines. It is suggested to the visitor to knock and inquire if they have a letter for him, and upon his supplying him with his name and address, he is himself, in due time, supplied with a packet (not pre-paid), which, on receiving, he finds filled with League tracts and other Free Trade publications. The scheme was so successful that the arrival of a 'foreign mail' was soon notified, and, of course, it brought with it a dispatch for every applicant, and at the foreign rate of postage."

Enough goods were left unsold at the bazar to furnish another very well-stocked and remunerative one at Manchester.

Protection to agriculture, freedom of trade, and the condition of the laboring classes, continually appeared on the surface of the debates during the session of 1845, and scarcely a week passed in which they were not incidentally discussed. A general discussion on the policy of the Protective Laws was raised by a motion proposed by Mr. Cobden on the 13th of March for a "select committee to inquire into the causes and extent of the alleged existing agricultural distress, and into the effects of legislative protection upon the interest of landowners, tenant-farmers, and farm la-

borers." He undertook to prove the existence
of distress among the farmers by quoting the
declarations of some of the highest authorities in
the agricultural interest; that half the farmers in
the country were in a state of insolvency, and
that the other half were paying rents out of their
capital, and fast hastening to the same melancholy
condition. This was, therefore, the proper time
for bringing on a motion for inquiry. The doubts
as to the cause of this distress were also sufficient
reasons for instituting it. Sir Robert Peel had
said that the distress was local, and did not arise
from legislation. Mr. Bankes, on the contrary,
maintained that the distress was general, and did
arise from legislation. It had also been said that
the Corn Law had been successful in keeping up
the price of corn; but to this it had been replied
that the price of wheat when the present Corn
Law was passed was 56s.—that it was now only
45s.—and that it would only be 35s. a quarter
next year if we had another plentiful harvest.
Under such circumstances, might it not be well to
inquire what was the benefit of protection? He
proceeded to show that the first great evil under
which the farmer labored was his want of capital.
The land required an expenditure of £10 an acre,
and had only £5 applied to it. Why could not
capital be profitably employed on the land? Because there was no security of tenure, and capital shrunk from insecurity of every sort. In En-

gland, leases were the exception, and he was sorry to say that farmers with leases were in a still worse condition than those who had them not; for the covenants in their leases were quite antediluvian, and were not fitted for the present state of agricultural science. He created much amusement by reading the covenants of a Cheshire lease, and contended that such covenants were nothing more than traps to catch the unwary, and fetters to bind the honest and intelligent. He advised the Anti-Corn-Law League to purchase a model farm, a model homestead, model cottages, and model gardens; but he would also have a model lease, and a farmer of intelligence, with sufficient capital. It was said that farmers would not now take leases. What did that mean? It meant that by the process which the landlords had adopted, they had rendered the farmers servile, and therefore not anxious to become independent. The cause of the want of capital and the insecurity of tenure was the Corn Laws. Free Trade in corn would be more beneficial to the farmers and the laborers than to any other class. Sir Robert Peel had recently admitted foreign fat cattle, but he refused to admit the raw material which was necessary to make cattle fat. He had absolutely reversed the course which Mr. Huskisson adopted with regard to manufactures. He maintained that all grazing and arable farmers were interested in having a large and cheap supply of provender. They were sending out vessels every day to Ichaboe for guano as manure, when the importation of cheap provender, which was now prohibited, would give every farmer a cheaper and more valuable species of manure, produced upon his farm. He described the lamentable condition of the laborers, and asked the landlords, after they had brought their dependents to so melancholy a state, whether they would be afraid to risk, he would not say this experiment, but this inquiry. Protection had been a failure when it reached a prohibitory duty of 80s.; it had been a failure when it reached the pivot price of 60s.; and it was a failure now, when they had got a sliding-scale, for they had admitted the lamentable condition of their tenantry and peasantry. He called upon all the gentlemen who entered the House, not as politicians, but as the farmers' friends, to support his motion, which was intended for their benefit, and not for their injury. The motion was, like its precursors, though ably supported by the present Earl Grey, then Lord Howick, and others, negatived by a considerable majority.

A great concession to the Free Trade cause was made in the course of this session. Lord John Russell brought forward a set of resolutions on the condition of the laboring classes. He stated that he could not now recommend the fixed duty of eight shillings which he had proposed in 1841. He supposed no one would propose a smaller duty than four shillings; he himself, if it were his affair, should propose one of four, five, or six shillings. Sidney Herbert, too, a member of the ministry, talked in terms of deprecation of the agricultural interest coming to Parliament "whining for protection." Cobden and the Free Traders made abundant use of this expression, which, if it implied any thing at all, involved their whole case and the justice of their claims. The farmers all over England read the reported expression—"whining for protection"—with dismay.

The Free Trade triumph was now fast approaching. Physical facts precipitated it. It remains for us to narrate with brevity the concluding act of that great drama in which Richard Cobden was the principal actor. The summer of 1845 was a continuous rainfall. The sun was scarcely seen from May until the summer of the succeeding year. Men began to fear for the harvest, and to calculate how much foreign dry wheat would be needed to mix with the English moist and soddened grain. Then it appeared that all over Europe the harvest would be a very deficient one, and dependence could only be placed on America. Another terrible calamity impended. Cottiers and market-gardeners began to notice brown spots appearing on the leaves of the potato plants. It appeared that this indication invariably proved that the roots were putrid and rotten. The League, the while, redoubled its exertions. They decreed a levy of £250,000, of which £62,000 were subscribed at one meeting. At a great demonstration in Manchester, in October, Mr. Cobden said there was only one remedy for the famine which threatened our island —only one means of averting the misery, starvation, and death of millions in Ireland. The ports must be opened. He referred to the rumors of a new Corn Law, and said that some delusive modification would be made unless the country declared against either a fixed duty or a reduced sliding-scale. He thus concluded: "We must not relax in our labors; on the contrary, we must be more zealous, more energetic, more laborious, than we ever yet have been. When the enemy is wavering, then is the time to press upon him. I call, then, on all who have any sympathy with our cause, who have any promptings of humanity, or who feel any interest in the well-being of their fellow-men, all who have apprehensions of scarcity and privations, to come forward to avert this horrible destiny—this dreadfully impending visitation."

Valuable accessions continued to be made to the League. Lord Ashley declared against the Corn Laws. Lord Morpeth joined the League. Lord John Russell wrote from Edinburgh to his constituents in the city of London a letter containing a complete recantation of his fixed-duty plan. Meanwhile the cabinet frequently met, and there were rumors of disagreements among its members. Sir Robert Peel and three of his colleagues wished to throw open the ports, but the majority of the ministers dissented, and he withdrew the proposition. On the 4th of December, the *Times* astounded the country by declaring that Parliament would be summoned in January for the purpose of repealing the Corn Laws. It was hotly and furiously assailed by the Tory prints, and its assertion flatly denied even by the papers generally believed to be admitted to the largest share of the confidence of ministers. But the *Times* quietly and pertinaciously adhered to and reiterated its statement: "We adhere," said the *Times*, "to our original announcement, that Parliament will meet early in January, and that a repeal of the Corn Laws will be proposed in one house by Sir Robert Peel, and in the other by the Duke of Wellington." It was believed that the duke had been most unwillingly, and at the last moment, persuaded by Peel, and only then by the statement of the premier that if he did not repeal the Corn Laws he must resign, and recommend her majesty to send for Mr. Cobden.

The royal speech at the opening of the session suggested an inquiry whether there might not still be a remission "of the existing duties upon many articles, the produce or manufacture of other countries." Large reductions in taxation on tallow, timber, silks, sugar, and other articles were announced. On the 27th of January, these remissions, and also the ministerial intentions with regard to the Corn Laws, were promulgated. Peel proposed to admit all agricultural produce used for cattle-feed duty free, colonial-grown wheat was to pay a mere nominal duty, and protection to cease totally in three years; the delay being granted to enable the farmers to arrange for the new state of things. In the interval, the duties would be materially reduced. The League at once gave their whole strength to the support of the scheme. Cobden appeared but seldom in the final Corn-Law debates of 1846. He had seriously impaired his health by his indefatigable exertions in the cause of cheap food, and he was frequently, especially just before the final triumph, absent from the House. In a great speech delivered in the course of the discussion which immediately followed the ministerial statement, he defended the policy of the League by which they had multiplied county voters by the purchase of freeholds, and the allocation of them in small lots. "Let it come to the worst," said he; "carry on the opposition to this measure for three years more; yet there is a plan in operation much maligned by some honorable gentlemen opposite, and still more maligned in another place, but which, the more the shoe pinches, and the more you wince at it, the more we like it out of doors. Now, I say, we have confronted this difficulty, and are prepared to meet it. We are calling into exercise the true old English forms of the Constitution of five centuries' antiquity, and we intend that the ancient forty-shilling freehold franchise shall countervail this innovation of yours in the Reform Bill. You think that there is something revolutionary in this. Why, you are the innovators and the revolutionists who introduced this new franchise into the Reform Bill. But I believe that it is perfectly understood by the longest heads among your party that we have a power out of doors to meet this difficulty. You should bear in mind that less than one half of the money invested in the savings' banks, laid out at a better interest in the purchase of freeholds, would give qualifications to more persons than your 150,000 tenant-farmers. But you say that the League is purchasing votes and giving away the franchise. No, no, we are not quite so rich as that; but be assured that if you prolong the contest for three or four years— which you can not do—if, however, it comes to the worst, we have the means in our power to meet the difficulty, and are prepared to use them."

With mingled ridicule and good-humor he described the various Protectionist terrors and delusions which still filled rural and Tory minds. He said, "The working-classes, not believing that wages rise and fall with the price of bread, when you tell them that they are to have corn at 25s. a quarter, instead of being frightened, are rubbing their hands with satisfaction. They are not frightened at the visions which you present to their eyes of a big loaf, seeing that they expect to get more money, and bread at half the price. And then the danger of having your land thrown out of cultivation! Why, what would the men in smock frocks in the south of England say to that? They would say, 'We shall get our land for potato-ground at a halfpenny a lug, instead of paying threepence or fourpence for it.' These fallacies have all been disposed of; and if you lived more in the world — more in contact with public opinion, and less within that charmed circle which you think the world, but which is really nothing but a clique; if you gave way less to the excitement of clubs—less to the buoyancy which arises from talking to each other as to the effect of some smart speech in which a minister has been assailed, you would see that it was mere child's play to attempt to baulk the intelligence of the country on this great question, and you would not have talked as you have talked for the last eleven days." Considerable majorities carried the bill through its varied stages, and it had passed the Lords ere the end of May.

Peel gracefully acknowledged the right of Cobden to be considered the real author of the measure: "The name which ought to be, and will be associated with the success of these measures, is the name of one who, acting, I believe, from pure and disinterested motives, has, with untiring energy, made appeals to our reason, and has enforced those appeals with an eloquence the more to be admired because it was unaffected and unadorned; the name which ought to be chiefly associated with the success of these measures is the name of RICHARD COBDEN."

The League had accomplished its work. It was formally dissolved at a great meeting at Manchester. Mr. Cobden addressed it, and congratulated his audience not only on the success achieved, but on the instruction communicated to the people, which would render it impossible ever again to impose the Corn Laws. Of Peel he said: "If he has lost office, he has gained a country. For my part, I would rather descend into private life with that last measure of his, which led to his discomfiture, in my hand, than mount to the highest pinnacle of human power." Referring to the labors of himself and his colleagues, he said: "Many people will think that we have our reward in the applause and *éclat* of public meetings; but I declare that it is not so with me, for the inherent reluctance I have to address public meetings is so great, that I do not even get up to present a petition to the House of Commons without reluctance. I therefore hope I may be believed when I say that if this agitation terminates now, it will be very acceptable to my feelings ; but if there should be the same necessity, the same feeling which impelled me to take the part I have taken, will impel me to a new agitation—ay, and with tenfold more vigor, after having had a little time to recruit my health." He moved "That, an Act of Parliament having been passed providing for the abolition of the Corn Laws in February, 1849, it is deemed expedient to suspend the active operation of the Anti-Corn-Law League; and the executive council in Manchester is hereby requested to take the necessary steps for making up and closing the affairs of the League with as little delay as possible." Mr. Bright seconded the resolution, and it was carried.

Mr. Prentice, himself one of the council of the League, says: "An air of grave solemnity had spread over the meeting as it drew to a close. There were five hundred gentlemen who had often met together during the great contest, and notwithstanding their exultation over a victory achieved, the feeling stole over their minds that they were never to meet again. Mr. Cobden reminded them that they were under obligations to the queen, who was said to have favored their cause as one of humanity and justice, and three hearty cheers in her honor loyally closed the proceedings."

CHAPTER VII.

FACTORY LEGISLATION.—THE TEN-HOURS' BILL.

WHAT has been called the "Condition of England Question" was being discussed all the time of the League agitation, and, indeed, both before and after it. Many different sects were there, and each one had quite as many leaders as the aggregate number of the sects. There were Chartists, and many ramifications of them; Socialists, not perhaps so divided, and although holding what society considers a more "leveling" opinion than even Chartism, yet composed of materials which were personally more respectable, and which have exercised collaterally much more important influences. Cobden's grand single-minded opinion among the rival doctors, as indeed has already sufficiently appeared in preceding pages, was, that the first thing was cheap bread (or, rather, this as the first fruits of farther Free Trade), and after that other matters might be considered. To Socialism he was ever opposed. Indeed, his cardinal doctrine of free, universal, and unrestricted competition is simply the direct antithesis of the cardinal doctrine of Socialism. Chartism in its rough form he never indicated any favor for. In fact, in his agitation he had fully as much trouble to encounter at the hands of the Chartists as any other class. At the same time, it must be admitted that his political opinions rested upon precisely the same radical foundation as Chartism, which is neither more nor less than the doctrine of the absolute political equality of every citizen, but without the admixture of any so-called "social" element.

From one phase of Chartism—or perhaps we should speak a little more accurately if we said from certain quondam Chartist leaders—sprang a definite public movement, in which afterward, strange to say, they found themselves associated with one of the proudest noblemen in England, and on which Mr. Cobden entertained, and expressed manfully, as was his wont, very definite opinions. Our elder readers, at least, will not need the information that we refer to the agitation about the Factory and Ten-Hours' Bill question. Perhaps we shall best economize our space, and at the same time conduce to clearness, if we leave Mr. Cobden and his views altogether out of sight for one or two pages, confine ourselves to the delineation of the opinions and proceedings of the friends of legislation in this direction, and then recur to Mr. Cobden, and discover his opinions, and the reasons he gave for them.

The year 1838 chronicled the avowed and open beginning of Chartism, when a great meeting, attended by 200,000 persons, was held on Kersal Moor, in Lancashire. The leaders of the Chartists in these early days were Stephens, a Wesleyan minister, who suffered eighteen months' imprisonment in Knutsford jail for certain incendiary expressions alleged to have been uttered by him on this occasion. Secondly, Feargus O'Connor, of whom Miss Martineau says—and we not only quote, but endorse her words—"It is very probable that from the moment when Feargus O'Connor first placed himself at the head of a Chartist procession to the last stoppage of his land scheme, he may have fancied himself a sort of savior of the working classes; but if so, he must bear the contempt and compassionate disapproval of all men of ordinary sense and knowledge, as the only alternative from their utter reprobation. Thirdly, Richard Oastler, a bland, hospitable, and generous-hearted Yorkshire "squire," as his adherents invariably called him, rather than a man fitted for popular leadership, but yet, above all others, the man most entitled to be considered the author of the Ten-Hours' Bill. Lastly, John Fielden, of Todmorden, also a man of bigger heart than head, although the latter was by no means deficient in capacity. The last two named dissociated themselves from Chartism whenever it began to be turbulent; Oastler being known as the advocate out of doors of a government bill for the compulsory limitation of the hours of labor

in factories to ten hours a day, while Fielden and
Lord Ashley, now Lord Shaftesbury, pleaded the
same cause on the floor of the House. But Fielden combined the two advocacies—in the House
and out of it. To narrate at any length the whole
history of the agitation would be to turn this biography—or at least a chapter of it—into a history. We only reproduce sufficient of its incidents to make the opinions of Mr. Cobden on the
question, subsequently to be adduced by us, sufficiently clear even to those whose first information on the subject is derived from these pages.

Lord Ashley had much support for his proposal
both in and out of the House. Such towns as
Manchester were placarded with bills with these
words: "Less Work! More Wages! Sign for
Ten Hours!" This was quite enough to raise
the enthusiasm of the operatives; and in the
two houses of Parliament some high Conserva-
tives believed in the bill because they believed
in the parental character of the government.
Some of the Radicals, again, went for it on the
ground that those poor who were not represented in the Legislature deserved, on that special
and peculiar ground, the protection of the state.
Others again—and probably a more numerous
constituent part of the supporters (we mean here,
of course, the upper-class supporters) of the bill
—supported it because it enabled them to annoy,
vilify, and defame the League, all of whom were

represented as the most horrid and hellish tyrants over their "hands." The members of the
League, and also many of the more sagacious of
the observant public, thought it somewhat strange
that Lord Ashley should develop so much humanity for Lancashire operatives whose families were
earning £3 per week, while his father's Dorset-
shire laborers received no more than 10s. It appeared, too, that he himself knew very little or
nothing of the vilified "manufacturing system,"
and was more than once made the dupe of the
vilest epistolary information. And in the vilifi-
cation of the manufacturers, or rather of the
Leaguers—for here lay the animus—the Ten-
Hours' Bill men either disdained not, or were to
their shame compelled to receive, the aid of the
most unscrupulous man who ever sat and shout-
ed in the English House of Commons, whose
name we will not here mention. The member to
whom we allude accused Mr. Cobden of paying
his hands on the Truck System—that is, of com-
pelling them to receive a portion of their wages
in goods, from which their master had a profit.
Cobden actually found it necessary—so hot was
the acrimony over the combined Corn-Law and
Ten-Hours controversy—to have the following
written voucher sent from his print-works, and he
read it in his place in the House:

"You are aware that our wages are paid every
Saturday morning, and our rule is that every per-

son in the works shall be paid by eight o'clock
with money, so that they can lay out their money
to the best advantage when and where they
please."

Even this denial did not suffice for the "honorable member." Eleven days after, "he asked Mr.
Cobden if he would deny that he kept cows, and
supplied the people with milk from them, deduct-
ing the amount from their wages?"

We tell the sequel exactly as it appears in
Hansard, with only the reservation which we
have already specified:

"Mr. Cobden. Does the honorable member
charge me with pursuing the Truck System?"

"Mr. ———— had said, 'Would the honorable
member deny it?' If he did, it was his duty to
take that denial; but he would give his reasons
for having asked the question, and his authority
for having done so."

"Mr. Cobden hoped that the House would give
him credit for not wishing to introduce personal
discussion into its debates. It seemed to him
that the statement which had gone abroad in the
Times as a charge against him was withdrawn.
He was not, therefore, directly called upon to answer it, but he would treat it as a charge made
against him last night which was not adhered to
to-day. If, however, the House would allow him,
he would state a few facts in reference to the
business with which he was connected. That

business could not be carried on without the consumption of large quantities of cow-dung. He
was now letting the honorable member for ———
into the arcana of the calico-printing trade. As
many hundred tons of dung were used in this
trade, it was necessary for manufacturers to keep
great numbers of cows. Now it so happened
that his printing-works being situated close to a
town, it was found more convenient to buy the
requisite quantity of dung than to keep cows, and,
therefore, the insinuations of the honorable member for ——— were not only untrue, but destitute of the shadow of a foundation. If the House
would allow him, he would remind it that those
charges were evidently got up for the purpose
of distracting the attention of the public from a
great and important question. He must confess
that he did not understand how the alleged mis-
conduct of mill-owners and manufacturers could
properly form a part of discussions on the Corn
Laws. If it was true, as the honorable member
for ——— had stated, that the master manufacturers were tyrants to their workmen, that could
be no reason why their sufferings should be added to by increasing the price of food."

It was only a very few persons indeed who
defended the Truck System. These few alleged
that there were exceptional occasions on which
it was an advantage to the operative; thus, where
places of marketing were distant, or, if accessible,

where the goods were inferior, it might be desirable that the master should become purveyor as well as employer. The obvious common-sense answer to this plea was, that the temptation to extortion was so great that it were better to get quit of the system altogether, than retain it on a pretext so illusory and so easily taken advantage of. For our purpose it is sufficient to remark, that Mr. Cobden's annoyance at the imputation was so evident as to prove irrefragably his detestation of the plan. With the Ten-Hour question the case was quite different. We have already indicated some of the pleas by which certain of the advocates of the legislative restriction of the hours of labor defended their position. The others we shall presently gather when we reproduce the pith of Mr. Cobden's counter-arguments. Meanwhile, it is merely necessary to allude to the steps connected with the passing of the various acts, and the nature of their provisions. The ultimate success of Lord Ashley's measure bade fair to be frustrated by disputes between the Churchmen and the Dissenters over clauses about the religious education of those whose hours of labor it was proposed to diminish. These at last were overcome, and, with the aid of the respective governments in office at the passing of the various acts, they were at last placed on the statute-book.

The Ten-Hours' Bill was passed in June, 1847,

while, as we shall see in the next chapter, Mr.
Cobden was out of England; it prescribes that
no person under the age of eighteen, and no female above the age of eighteen, shall be employed
in any factory for more than ten hours in one day,
nor for more than fifty-eight in any one week.
A supplementary act prescribed that no such
child or female should work before six A.M., or
after six P.M.; or, if so, only to recover lost time,
and then not after seven. There were other reg-
ulations about meal-times, fencing of machinery,
etc. A previous act, that of 1844, had already
enacted that certain hours should be reserved for
education, and that no children under ten should
work in textile factories.

It will be at once seen that on the main question, namely, the limitation of the hours of labor
of adults, whether in factories or elsewhere, Mr.
Cobden's views have not to this day been legis-
latively reversed, with this exception, that mills
can not be kept going without juvenile aid. It
will be enough, therefore, if we give merely in
two or three sentences the gist of one speech as
sample of others delivered by him, in which he
opposed Lord Ashley's Ten-Hours' Bill: He ridiculed the idea that for ten hours' work a man
could earn more than he could for twelve. And
if that were so, the loss of two hours' pay would
be a more serious injury than the saving of two
hours' work. People were generally paid in the

cotton districts by the piece. How, then, could such legislation affect them favorably, so far as wages were concerned? It had been said that the manufacturers could so increase the speed of their machinery as that the same work might be done as heretofore in twelve hours. He had made inquiries, and found that precisely the contrary was the case. There was a tendency to diminish speed, for the high rate of speed at which they had been working caused more loss in waste than saving in wages. The other argument, which cut the ground entirely from the former, was, that diminished production would give farther employment to labor, and cause one sixth more mills to be built. On the contrary, the fact was, our present sale of cotton goods arose from and was owing to their cheapness. If we increased our prices we should lose our customers, and in foreign countries the handloom, distaff, and spindle would be once more at work. The only real way to shorten the hours of labor was to remove the restrictions on industry. He did not mean by that to say, as had been said by others, that a reduction in the price of bread would alone afford compensation to the laboring classes for a reduction in the hours of labor; he did not see in the mere reduction in the price of wheat, or sugar, or coffee, the great means of enabling the operatives to get on with fewer hours of labor. "But," said he, "if we enlarged the various

markets for our productions, if we allowed a full
and free exchange of our commodities for the
corn, and sugar, and coffee of other countries, this
would be the practical means of raising the practical value of our products, and consequently of
raising the value of the labor which produced
them; so that, indeed, ten hours' labor might be
as good or better than twelve hours' now for the
pocket of the laborer, and produce as much profit
to the employer."

Thus it clearly appears Mr. Cobden was not
against ten hours' labor in itself, or, indeed, any
prudent and possible reduction of the hours of labor.   In fact, this very condition, which he pre-
dicted in 1844, in these last sentences, as rendering a reduction of labor possible and advisable,
had come about—through him more than all other men put together—some years ere he died.
And many facts around us to-day, both in the labor market and the food market, prove to us that
both his wishes were fulfilled, namely, the attainment of the end which he approved and desired,
and the adoption of the proper method of seeking after it.

CHAPTER VIII.

PEACE, RETRENCHMENT, AND REFORM.

THE devotion with which Mr. Cobden entered into the Free Trade agitation had been most injurious to his own personal and pecuniary interests. He had separated from his early partners, and associated with himself his brothers, who continued the printing works at Chorley. Miss Martineau sets down his clear money loss at £20,000; and we think the estimate a very moderate one. A very short time before the final triumph of his efforts, he had resolved to retire from the agitation and devote himself to retrieve the fortunes of his business. He actually wrote to Mr. Bright, who was in Scotland at the time, declaring this intention. Mr. Bright at once hastened to Manchester, to urge his friend to reconsider his determination; and he succeeded. We have seen that it was Cobden who enlisted Bright as his chief lieutenant in the cause. He brought him into the ranks at the beginning of the contest; Bright succeeded in keeping Cobden to his post on the verge of its termination. The council of the League, and the Free Traders generally, determined, when their labors were done and their organization dissolved, to mark in a substantial

DUNFORD HOUSE.

way not only their sense of Cobden's services, but their acknowledgment of the pecuniary sacrifices which they had involved.   The munificent sum of £80,000 was subscribed and presented to Cobden, it being understood that by thus securing his independence he would be enabled to relinquish his business connections, and devote those energies which had already done so much for the land to the general work of legislation and statesmanship.   A portion of this fund was applied to the purchase of the house in which Cobden was born, and a small estate surrounding it.   It was understood that he invested a large portion of the balance in American railway securities.   For some years they were unremunerative; and many impertinent and offensive statements, chiefly emanating from the monopolist regions against which Cobden had employed his victorious lance, were made about a man who undertook to manage a nation's affairs not being able to control his own, and the like.   It was even gravely argued that Mr. Cobden had not a right to do as he would with his own; and he was reproached by persons who had not contributed one penny toward the testimonial fund for having employed his money in any other way than in investments native to the English soil.   About fifteen years after the date at which we have arrived in our narrative, while Cobden was absent from England, seeking a restoration of his health in Algeria, a few gentlemen, without making any public appeal, subscribed among themselves a sum stated at the time to amount to £40,000, with the purpose of requesting Mr. Cobden's acceptance of it as a supplementary offering to that formerly contributed. The *Times*, with extremely questionable taste, came out with a leading article, in which this intention was announced, and indulging generally in a sneering and contemptuous tone. This article was, we believe, the first announcement to Cobden himself of the purpose of his admirers. He at once wrote home, stating that under no circumstances could he accept the proposed gift. We are glad to observe, as we prepare these sheets, that a movement has been successfully made at Manchester to raise £20,000 as a national tribute to Mr. Cobden's memory, the sum to be settled upon his widow and daughters. It is only just to Mr. Cobden's reputation as a man capable of guiding his own affairs to add, that we believe—and we derive our belief from authorities whom we accept as perfectly competent—that Mr. Cobden's American investment, which was in bonds or other securities of the Illinois Central Railway, had turned out to be productive for some time before his death. The investment now yields six per cent. return, and will, doubtless, as the population and traffic of that fertile Western state are augmented, become still more productive.

The next few years of Mr. Cobden's life present

him, in Parliament and out of it, with his tongue constantly, and occasionally with his pen, as the consistent supporter of peace, reform, retrenchment, and the introduction of arbitration, instead of war, as the accepted settler of international difficulties. After the Free Trade triumph he sought a season of repose. His health had given way, and he repaired to the Continent to seek its restoration. Ere he departed Lord John Russell offered him a seat in the cabinet, but he declined it. He visited in succession France, Spain, Italy, Germany, and Russia. Wherever he went he was most warmly received. Complimentary banquets were got up, and the warmest eulogies passed upon the great breaker-down of the rivalries of nations by the most distinguished men of their respective countries. In his absence there was a general election. He was returned for the West Riding as well as for Stockport, and chose the more distinguished seat. He came back to England in time to contribute his valuable co-operation to the government of Lord John Russell in their extension of the principle of Free Trade to sugar and the navigation laws, and other minor sources of the revenue. After an absence of his name from the pages of *Hansard* for a twelvemonth, we find him in the spring of 1848 breaking ground again by supporting Mr. Labouchere's proposal for the repeal of the navigation laws. The old principles were brought up afresh, the application of them only being different. He showed, by an appeal to the published evidence, that we can build ships better than foreign countries, and at as cheap a rate; sail them as well; take greater care of the cargoes, and secure greater punctuality and dispatch. The only drawbacks were of a moral kind — insubordination and drunkenness; but they would yield to better culture. He repudiated the boastful language which he so often heard respecting England's naval supremacy. He must say that those boasts were generally uttered after dinner, and therefore they might be the result of a little extra excitement. The abolition of the navigation laws would not affect the naval condition of Great Britain. But was this a time to be always singing "Rule Britannia?" If honorable members opposite had served with him on the Committee on the Army, Navy, and Ordnance Estimates, they would have a just sense of the cost of that song. The constant assertion of maritime supremacy was calculated to provoke kindred passions in other nations; whereas, if Great Britain enunciated the doctrines of peace, she would invoke similar sentiments from the rest of the world. Mr. Disraeli made a sarcastic reply, in which he, with some humor, stated that he would not sing "Rule Britannia" for fear of distressing Mr. Cobden, but he did not think the House would encore "Yankee Doodle."

About this time the nation got into one of its extraordinary panics about a French invasion. A letter by the Duke of Wellington, addressed to Sir John Burgoyne, in which the old warrior advocated the enrollment of militia to the number of 150,000, and other costly measures of precaution, was made public. Lord Ellesmere and others joined in the cry. Cobden chose the occasion of a great Free Trade demonstration at Manchester about the navigation laws to show the unreal foundation of the alarm. His speech was unusually jocular, as these sentences will testify: "Are the French, or the majority of them, thieves, pickpockets, and murderers? If they were, could they exist as an organized community — a community as orderly as ours? for we have had as little tumult in France during the last five or six years as in England. I see another paper in London, a weekly paper, the editor of which used to write with some degree of gravity, but I suppose that he is so panic-stricken that he has lost all his wits; that paper tells us that the next war with France will be made without a declaration of war, and that truly we have to protect our queen at Osborne House against those ruffianly Frenchmen, who may come without notice and carry off her majesty. What a lesson has our courageous queen read to such people as those! She went over to France unattended, unprotected, and threw herself upon the shore there at the

Chateau d'Eu, literally in a bathing-machine. Now there is either great courage on the one side, or great cowardice on the other. / But this is a sort of periodical visitation that we have. I sometimes compare it to the cholera, for I believe the last infliction we had of this kind came about the time of the cholera; and then we were to have had an invasion from the Russians, as our friend has told you. I am rather identified with and interested in that apprehended invasion, for it was that which first made me an author and a public man—and I believe it is quite possible, if it had not been for the insanity on the part of some of our newspapers—and some of them that are now just as insane—who told us that the Russians were coming, some foggy day, to land near Yarmouth—if it had not been for that insanity on the part of some of our newspapers, I should not have turned author, written pamphlets, or become a public man, and I might have been a thrifty, painstaking calico-printer to this day."

In this year, for the first time since the commencement of his career in Parliament, Mr. Cobden pronounced in his place in the House opinions decidedly favorable to the causes of large electoral reform, secret voting, and the shortening of the duration of Parliaments. The occasion was a general motion by Mr. Hume, comprising all these suggested improvements. Cobden was one of the chief speakers in the debate which ensued. He had refused, it will be recollected, so long as he believed the Corn Laws to be the crying evil of the country, to mix up the Reform, or any other question, with the advocacy of Free Trade. Even when his warm friend and ally, Joseph Sturge, proposed to combine the extended suffrage with the Anti-Corn-Law questions, Cobden, while not discouraging him, elected for himself to devote himself exclusively to his first line.   Now that his efforts in this field were successful, he was consistently free to allot due prominence to his views on Parliamentary Reform.   His response was most ample and loyal whenever challenged to show his real colors.

Mr. Hume's motion came on on the 20th of June.   It had been previously set down for the 23d of May.   But when the worthy economist of Montrose rose in his place after eleven o'clock on the night of that day, he craved leave to postpone his motion on account of the lateness of the hour. Feargus O'Connor, in his mad way, insisted on the debate being inaugurated and proceeded with. When he sat down, Mr. Cobden rose, and addressed the House for a few minutes.   We hold his speech to be eminently worthy of entire reproduction, for it is not only important as an autobiographical and also an historical utterance; not only is it peculiarly illustrative of the wise, cautious, and conservative element in Cobden's character, but it is worthy of transfer to our pages for present political use in our own days.

"My conviction is that there can be but one opinion on the part of every sincere, honest, and intelligent man in the country, that the honorable member for Montrose is entirely blameless for the delay which has taken place in the discussion of his motion. I think that no reasonable man would suppose that any one having to conduct so important a question would bring it before the House at a quarter past eleven o'clock. The object of my honorable friend is that this question may be fully discussed; and if it had begun at five o'clock, I doubt whether one evening would have sufficed for a full discussion of it. The honorable gentleman who has just spoken has undertaken to give advice, in no very courteous or complimentary terms, to my honorable friend; but if I were to venture to give my honorable friend advice, it would be this—that in conducting this important question, he should not follow the advice, still less the example, of the honorable member who calls himself the leader of the working classes of this country, but who, after undertaking for nine years to lead them in the advocacy of what is called 'The People's Charter'—[Mr. F. O'Connor: Fifteen years]—who, as the honorable gentleman stated the other day at a meeting of his convention, had, after, as he now says, fifteen years of leadership and advocacy of the

'People's Charter,' met with but one man in the House of Commons upon whom, in his absence, he could depend for the advocacy of his principles. ['Name.']   I can not name the honorable member; but I think that is sufficient to warn the honorable member for Montrose to beware how he conforms himself to the tactics and advice coming from the honorable member for Nottingham.   I think, if any thing could open the eyes of the working classes of the country to a just sense of the value of the honorable member for Nottingham's services, it is the position in which he has been placed by every honorable member, except one, in this House, after fifteen years of leadership.   I have had long experience of that honorable member, and perhaps he will not accuse me of being actuated by any feelings of hostility toward him—for certainly no honorable member has lavished so many compliments upon me as he has done—but I say, that my experience of the conduct of the honorable member out of this House, and of the spirit and manner in which he has tried to array the working classes against every man who could effectually assist them in carrying forward the objects in which the honorable member himself professed to wish them success, convinces me that he has done more to retard the political progress of the working classes of England than any other public man that ever lived in this country.   I speak from

L

long experience of that honorable member; and
no man has more right to speak of him than I
have upon that subject. For seven years I had
the direct and relentless hostility of that honorable member upon what, I believe, was strictly a
question affecting the interests of the working
classes of this country—I mean the abolition of
the tax upon their food. That honorable gentleman did all he could to array the working classes
against me, and against those who acted with me.
I had more hostility to encounter from that honorable member than from the Duke of Buckingham and all his party. And what is the result?
I never fraternized with the honorable gentleman or his myrmidons. No one can for a moment charge me with ever having done so. I
always treated the honorable member as the leader of a small, insignificant, and powerless party.
I never identified him or his party with the
working class of this country. I ever treated
him, as I do now, not as the leader of the working classes, but as the leader of a small and organized faction. I have set the honorable gentleman publicly at defiance, and all his followers;
and I never failed to beat them by votes whenever
I met them at public meetings in the open air in
any county in England. In any advocacy I may
enter upon for the working classes, as I never
have, so I never will, offer to fraternize with the
honorable member and his organized followers;

and if he says, as he has said, that he is preparing his followers to go along with us, I say to him again, that with him and his Chartists, as an organized body, I never will fraternize. I have set them at defiance before, and I set them at defiance now. I would advise my friend, the honorable member for Montrose, not to be deluded by any thing which may fall from the honorable member as to the power he has over the working classes of this country. He was weak before, he is harmless now; and whatever he may threaten or promise will be equally powerless and uninfluential. Ferocious as was his attack upon my honorable friend, the member for Montrose, there is no one who will not be as well disposed as ever to continue to my honorable friend that confidence which he has always enjoyed from the great mass of the people of this country."

Mr. Cobden was of course a strenuous supporter of Mr. Henry Berkeley's annual motions on the Ballot. His precise views on this important political question of the secondary grade may be gathered from a summary, contained in a few sentences of a brief speech delivered by him in the same year, in reply to Lord John Russell. He said that he viewed the question of the Ballot with less interest than he had done twelve years previously. Had it been then adopted, it would have done much to put an end to that corruption

in the boroughs and subserviency in the counties
which they had now to deplore; but it was too
late now to remedy the evil, excepting by an in-
fusion of new blood into the constituency. Still,
he believed the ballot was the best mode of taking the vote in this or any country, and he should
vote for the question. The question must be on
its last legs when no better answer could be made
to it than that furnished by Lord John. Secret
voting, his lordship said, was opposed to the "open
and free constitution of the country." The mode
of election was open, but was it free? A jury
gave its verdict openly; but the analogy was unfortunate; for, though a jury must be unanimous
when it convicted, it was not necessary that it
should be so when it did not, nor were the votes
of each juror published. The grand jury was a
secret tribunal. In Scotland, where the verdict
depended upon the majority, there was no publicity of the votes of the jurors. The analogy of
the open voting in the House of Commons did
not apply either; for members went there to perform, by delegation, certain duties for their constituents, and they were held responsible for their
acts; or why were they subject to periodical election? (The following, we think, was a most happy and apposite thrust.) "And how are the constituencies to form a judgment upon them if they
do not know what they have done? But are the
electors responsible to non-electors? If they are,

then the non-electors must be competent to judge
of the way in which the trust is exercised, and
this is an argument for extending the suffrage to
them." It was, he said, for the sake of the counties in particular that he wished to see the Ballot
carried into effect; for he believed that if the county constituencies possessed the Ballot, they would
send some of the best representatives which the
country afforded to that House; and he wanted
to see the farmer class in this country men of more
character, dignity, and self-respect than they ever
could be under the existing degrading system.

We return to that class of topics which constituted the subjects of nine tenths of Mr. Cobden's
public appearances in the years intervening between the termination of the Anti-Corn-Law
struggle and the commencement of the Crimean
War. During these years Cobden introduced
annual, or oft-repeated motions in the House of
Commons, seeking to bind that body to the af-
firmation of these principles: that the national
expenditure might be with prudence and safety
so far reduced as to admit of a reduction of ten
millions of taxation, and that the stipulation of arbitration should be introduced in all international
treaties. As means to the advocacy of these ends,
he made some use of the press, and large use of
the platform, and threw himself heart and soul
into the operations of the Peace Society; but
he always carefully guarded himself against the

imputation of being a " Peace-at-any-price man."
While another great panic of a French invasion
existed in this country in the early part of 1853,
Cobden said, "It was not newspaper articles, or
speeches made, but our great naval preparations,
which really endangered our understanding with
France, and caused uneasiness at home. If a
friendly note were to be exchanged with the
French government on the subject, he had no
doubt that it would be responded to in a manner
that would banish all suspicion. *If it did not,
he would be ready to vote £100,000,000 to resist
a French invasion.*"   And more recently, while,
it will be remembered, he resisted a vote of
£2,000,000 for the defense of certain of our arsenals by stone fortifications, he said, if he really
thought they were needed and would answer, he
would say, "Take twenty, not two millions."

Early in 1849 Cobden proposed his two resolutions relating to the arbitration clause and the
ten million reduction of revenue and expenditure.
The unfortunately depressed state of the revenue
gave the question of financial reform a very strong
hold on the public mind. Associations advocat-
ing retrenchment were formed in many of the
great towns, and Cobden was sanguine that he
could cut down the expenditure, if not quite to
that of the normal year of Whig economic administration—1835—at least to a considerably lower
point than that at which it stood in 1848, and the

subsequent years in which he renewed his resolution. His great points were that the agricultural interest, which again complained of special burdens, could only expect to be relieved of them if it united with the economists in pruning the expenditure; that the navy was our true line of defense, and that we might with perfect safety largely reduce our military establishments and costs; and that the colonies should defray the expenses of the maintenance of their own governments and external defense. In the latter view he was well sustained by Sir William Molesworth, who made this question his specialty as much as Cobden had made Free Trade his. It is now universally recognized by all parties as axiomatic, although as yet it is rather theoretically than practically incorporated in our colonial policy.

Mr. Cobden's exertions in this direction were far from fruitless. Ere the close of the period of his public life now under our consideration, an offensive Militia Bill had to be withdrawn; and although Prince Louis Napoleon had been elected President of the French Republic, ministers came before Parliament with the declaration that "large reductions had been made in the estimates of last year." Cobden had written, ere this, gleefully to his trusty abettor, Joseph Sturge—"I have been delighted with the success of your meetings. You Peace people seem to be the only men who have courage just now to call a public meeting. I always say that there is more real pluck in the ranks of the Quakers than in all our regiments of redcoats. . . . What progress has been made in public opinion during the last twelve months! Much of it is due to the efforts of your Peace Society. In fact, all good things pull together. Free Trade, peace, financial reform, equitable taxation, all are co-operating toward a common object."

. Thus modestly did Cobden write, disclaiming all credit himself, of "you Peace people," and "your Peace Society." He was himself not the least active, and certainly far from the least influential, of its members. The successive annual Peace Congresses—unhappily interrupted by the Crimean War, and by the bath of blood through which some leading portion of the human race has had to wade ever since—now in India, again in Italy, in Poland, in the Scandinavian Peninsula, and in the New World—were held successively at Brussels, Paris, Frankfort, London, Manchester, and Edinburg. Cobden was present as a leading speaker at all of them save the first, at which, however, a long letter from his pen was read. At Paris he said, to meet certain objections to his arbitration plan, "We do not propose to constitute the executive department of government arbitrators in difficulties between nations. We should wish to appoint arbitrators to suit each particular case; for instance, in a

question of naval or military etiquette, a general
or an admiral might be selected ; in a commercial matter, a merchant, and so on." About the
same time, in his place in Parliament, he reminded members of a number of instances in which,
during fifty years previously, commissioners had
been employed to adjust disputes between nations, and in no instance had such arbitration led
to war. There was, therefore, nothing either vis-
ionary or novel in his plan. In fact, Mr. Cobden's
arbitration scheme and proposed reduction of national expenditure were not only very much more
practicable than was generally held — and if admitted to be practicable, there could be no doubt
of their high utility—but the principles of the
Peace Society, of which Cobden was not ashamed
to constitute himself the champion and exponent,
were very different from the popular but erroneous idea of them. On this point, the English
mob (we include all classes of it) accepted their
idea of what the Peace Society really was, not
from its own annual and authorized documents,
or from the explicit and definitely limited statements of men like Cobden, but from the representations of fanatics and lampooners. It was
not the object of the Peace Society to proclaim
the advent of a millennium, but rather to provide,
during any intervals of peace which the world
might enjoy, practical measures to be used in lieu
of the sword in the contingency of future dis-

putes. Such measures were, reduction of armaments, arbitration, treaties, the propaganda of the doctrine of non-intervention, the development of all means of international communication—cheap postage, similarity of standards of weight, measure, and value. These proposals, and strenuous measures to band together in their support all Christian ministers and men, and all teachers of youth, and the consideration of the best and quickest means of effecting them, were the objects of Cobden and the Peace Society. His avowal of sympathy and identity with its precepts and purposes was the only aspect of his life that ever exposed him to ridicule, however he may have been, in other points of his belief, subjected to acrimony. We are, however, strongly inclined to believe that future generations will laud Cobden more highly for his devotion to this cause than for all his Free Trade triumphs, signal and extraordinary as these were.

CHAPTER IX.

THE LAST OF THE PEACE SOCIETY CONFERENCES.

THE writer of these pages has a vivid recollection of the appearance of Mr. Cobden at the very last of these Peace Conferences, which was held at Edinburg at the latter end of the autumn of 1853. Here Cobden had decidedly the laugh on his side. Early in that year, England had been in one of her periodical fears of a French invasion. Thrice within the limits of a very few years had this panic reappeared: when Prince de Joinville was young and bellicose; when the Duke of Wellington wrote his alarmist letter to Sir John Burgoyne; and at the close of 1852 and in the early part of 1853. Cobden had done all he could to abate the latter, as he had the former panics. So strongly had he felt on the subject at the beginning of this year as to publish his well-known pamphlet, " 1793 and 1853, in three letters, by R. Cobden." On the title-page he placed a somewhat scandalous and most naïve and candid quotation from Alison, referring to the former period —1793: " The passions were excited; democratic ambition was awakened; the desire of power under the name of Reform was rapidly gaining ground among the middle ranks, and the institutions of the country were threatened with an overthrow as violent as that which had recently. taken place in the French monarchy. In these circumstances, the only mode of checking the evil was by engaging in a foreign contest, by drawing off the ardent spirits into active service, and, in lieu of the modern desire for innovation, arousing the ancient gallantry of the British nation." This sentence being taken as a text by Cobden, he applied in his pamphlet the various lessons of English policy in 1793, and the costly results which succeeded it, to the requirements of 1853. A large portion of the public, in the midst of their war fever, not only refused to be convinced by it, but made it the special object of their ridicule. *Punch* caught the vulgar feeling, and executed a cartoon of Mr. Cobden, with long asinine ears, looking with a vacuous look into the muzzle of a cannon, and asserting that it was innocuous.

By the time the Peace Conference was in session in Edinburg, in October, all was changed. Mr. Cobden had now fairly the laugh against his decriers, for Nicholas had crossed the Pruth, fairly commenced his aggression upon Turkey—having been doubtless largely induced so to do by the conviction that England and France were quite alienated, and would not unite to resist his encroachment. And England and France were in close and friendly alliance. Mr. Cobden thus, at

Edinburg, took advantage of the turning of the tables, delivering this portion of his address with infinite humor and *verve :*

" The very minister who talked of the French coming from Cherbourg in one night, with 60,000 men, to invade our coasts, I myself heard say that, now the French and English are united, and have one common bond of interest, and are united by sentiments of mutual confidence and esteem, they are a power against whom it is in vain for Russia to contend; for all Europe would be powerless against such an irresistible combination.   (Hear, hear, and great applause.)   And what did I hear at the end of last session of Parliament in the queen's speech, as if it was to give to the Peace Party the climax of your triumph?   Not only does the queen in her speech, in Parliament, ere it separated, declare that she is on the best terms of amity with the French nation, but she rather goes out of the way to add that she is also on the best possible footing with the Emperor of the French.   (Laughter.)   Now I have often thought of supposing the case of an individual who had been ordered away from this country, as many persons are, for the benefit of their health, and supposing he had left our shores last January to take a voyage to Australia, returning again without remaining there, merely making the circuit of the globe for the benefit of his health.   He left England preparing her militia and fortifying her coasts, general officers writing to me offering to lay a wager that the French would come and invade us. (Loud laughter and cheers.) And he saw an inspector of cavalry and artillery moving about the Southern coasts, deputations from the railway companies waiting upon the Admiralty and the Ordnance to see how soon the Commissariat and the Ordnance supplies could be transmitted from the Tower to Dover or to Portsmouth; he left in the midst of all these preparations for the French invasion; he makes the circuit of the globe, and as he could see no newspaper—for one great motive in sending a careworn individual on such a voyage is to keep him away from politicians and the Post-office— he knows nothing of what has occurred during his absence. Well, he lands here in September, and the first thing he reads of in the newspapers is, that the French and English fleets are lying side by side in Besika Bay. He immediately says that there is to be a great battle—(laughter)—he turns to the leading article of the very paper that has told him before he left the country that the French emperor was a brigand and a pirate, and that the French people were about to invade England without notice or declaration of war—he turns to a leader in this paper—the very first he has seen after he has arrived in England—and there he finds that the English and French are so cordially united that their fleets are lying in

Besika Bay, under the command of Admiral Dundas; that we are prepared, if necessary, to send an army to be put under a French general, and that we are going into action, probably to-morrow, with the Russian fleet. Now the first thing that he would naturally ask would be this—'But can you trust this individual, whom, when I left Britain, you were characterizing as a brigand and a pirate? (Hear, hear.) What has happened? Has any thing happened to prove that these Peace people have been right and that you were wrong? What change has taken place? What does this mean? What guarantee has this man given you that when you go into action with the Russian fleet, he has not previously come to an understanding with the Emperor of Russia, and that, instead of joining you in firing broadsides into the Russian fleet, he will not join Russia in demolishing yours? (Hear, hear, and loud cheers.) And then, unless he has undergone a great change, and you have not explained to me how it happened, what proofs have you that when he has joined the Russian fleet, he will not come and ravage your coasts, burn down your houses, seize the Bank, and carry off the queen?'" (Loud laughter.)

But the most extraordinary effect of all was produced by this retort upon *Punch*—the delight and excitement of the audience (let it be remembered, no vulgar rabble, but a morning audience of one of the most intelligent cities in the empire) being something indescribable.

"Why, don't you remember the caricature in which your humble servant was represented with very long ears, thus (erecting his hands on each side of his head, amidst loud laughter), because he stood up and declared that he did not believe that the French were coming to invade us? Who has got the long ears and the fool's cap now?" (Roars of laughter.)

The proceedings of the Peace Conference at Edinburg consisted of three meetings (two morning and one evening) of the society, sitting as a society (to which, however, the general public were also admitted), and a public meeting, supposed to be entirely composed of persons who indicated by their presence neither that they agreed with nor differed from the principles of the society. At that meeting an amusing and stirring incident occurred, of which the writer had also the good fortune to be a spectator. He had accompanied to the platform an aged relative—one of the Edinburg committee for the reception of the delegates—and sat in one of the back seats immediately behind the chairman, Mr. Duncan McLaren, at that time chief magistrate of the city. He saw, to his surprise, that the seat of honor immediately on the left of the chair was reserved for a gentleman whose face he did not recognize as belonging to any one who had appeared at all at any of the previous meetings of the Conference. This gentleman pushed his way in a somewhat rough and unceremonious manner to his place, and his arrival created no little stir among the occupants of the platform, who were composed in almost equal proportions of Peace Society delegates from various parts, and of persons of all degrees of local importance. It was evident, however, by the courteous attentions paid to this gentleman, ere the opening of the meeting, by the chairman and others, that he was "somebody." Nevertheless, his appearance belied the idea of his importance which was produced by the attentions paid him. Neither laundress, perruquier, nor tailor seemed to any large extent to have been taken into consultation as to the preparation of his outer man; nor did the few words that fell from his lips in answer to the courtesies and greetings which he received indicate that either his instructors in his early life or himself at its later periods had bestowed much attention upon the graces, or even the proprieties of his diction. The then spectator and present narrator was mystified. And this mystification lasted some time—lasted through the chairman's opening speech; through the reading by Mr. Richard, the Secretary of the Society, of the list of the resolutions passed at the Conference; through an eloquent address by Elihu Burritt, and through another, overflowing with the rich-

M

est humor, by the late esteemed Rev. John Burnet, of Camberwell, one of the great representative Nonconformist leaders of our century. Then rose Mr. Cobden. He had not spoken long before the mystery was solved. "I am glad," said he, " on this occasion, that we have a gallant gentleman with us—if he will allow me, I will call him my gallant friend, for we have walked into the same lobby generally, if not always, when we were in the House of Commons together—we have a gallant officer here, who, if ever you have to fight instead of arbitrating,.will do your business as well as any body you can find. This gallant gentleman—this gallant admiral—has come from London, warm from the City of London Tavern, bringing with him a spirit impatient for some decisive proceedings in this troubled Eastern Question."

All at once it flashed upon the narrator's memory that, a week or two before, Sir Charles Napier had announced his intention, at a London Tavern meeting, of " bearding the Peace Society in its den," or some such phrase, which in the lapse of years has escaped our memory. This had been generally put down as a flourish of trumpets. But no ; here was the hero of Acre presented to our gaze, and—what was even better for juvenile hot blood, the prospect of a set-to between " Old Charley" and the great Peace heroes. " What a pity," thought we, " that Cobden speaks before him!" But when we heard Mr. Bright reply to the admiral, our regret vanished. The audience received all three with equal good humor, and with an equal share of plaudits —a circumstance not so much, perhaps, to be attributed to any vacillation or fickleness of the *popularis aura* as to a just and fair determination to give equal justice. Cobden's speech was diversified by occasional gruffly given interruptions from the admiral, most of which, however, were inaudible.

"The gallant gentleman," continued Mr. Cobden, "has declared his disapproval of the course we have taken, and I have no doubt that he has come here to state the grounds on which that disapprobation rests; and I should only be anticipating the duty which the right honorable chairman here can perform as well as any man in Scotland—I mean, in offering him, in their name, a most courteous reception and a most patient hearing for all that he may have to address to this meeting. My gallant friend says to me just now (alluding to one of the, to us, inaudible, or rather undistinguishable interruptions), 'How do you know I am your opponent?' I have no doubt, before we have done with him, we will make him an ally. That will be our business to-night. He is worth converting, I assure you."

Mr. Cobden went at length into the elucidation of those views upon land and maritime armaments which he had elaborated still more fully in the House of Commons in more recent years, and to which reference will be made in a succeeding chapter; told Sir Charles that "what he had heard people say, and what he had read in some of the prints in the Reform Club, about the objects of the Peace Conference, were pure fictions; and he would tell him what they really were;" and urged (in view of the then threatening Russian War) that for us, who had just been guilty of an atrocious encroachment upon the Burmese, "to pretend to exercise God's vengeance upon other nations of the world was presumption and hypocrisy."

One passage of Mr. Cobden's speech must be given at length, for it is explanatory and expository of a well-known saying of his, which has been intentionally misrepresented in some quarters, and ignorantly misapprehended in others:

"Our gallant visitor here, I see, referred, rather peculiarly, at the London Tavern, to a phrase that fell from me some years ago at a meeting, with regard to crumpling up the Russian Empire. Now the phrase I used was at a meeting on the subject of the Hungarian invasion in 1849. I attended a meeting in the City of London Tavern to protest against the invasion of Hungary by Russia. Russia was allowed then to march her armies across the territory of Turkey, through Wallachia and Moldavia, to strike a death-blow at the heart of Hungary, and no protest was ever recorded by our government against that act. And it is my deliberate conviction, from a patient study of the Blue-books—and it is the conviction of the most illustrious men who were engaged in that Hungarian struggle — that if Lord Palmerston had made but a simple verbal protest, in energetic terms, Russia would never have invaded Hungary by passing through the Moldavian and Wallachian territories. It is well known that the ministers of the Czar almost went down on their knees to beg and entreat him not to embark in a struggle between Austria and Hungary. Our protest would immediately have been backed by the ministry of the Czar if it had been made; and I believe it would have prevented that most atrocious outrage, as I consider it, upon the rights and liberties of a constitutional country. I said on that occasion, in the midst of all the excitement and frenzy that then prevailed in favor of Hungarian nationality, that I would resist any attempt to send an English force to fight the battles of Hungary on the banks of the Danube or the Theiss. I proclaimed the same thing then that I proclaim now. I did not disguise my views on the subject any more than I disguise my views now with regard to the conduct of Russia toward Turkey; but I said I will remain content with uttering my reprobation of the act. I would not sanction the sending of English soldiers and sailors to fight these distant battles. In fact, in a word, my opinions and my principles resolve themselves into this, that I will never argue for any battle whatever as to which I am not prepared to go and take a part in it. I would never send men to some distant part of the world without partaking of their peril; whenever a battle is to be fought with my consent, it shall be one in which I am willing to take a part myself. Well, I took occasion then, speaking in the City of London Tavern, to say that Russia did not contemplate attacking us; that if Russia did attack us, such were the great resources of this country —such were the enormous resources of wealth, and the scientific appliances which might be used for the purpose of naval warfare and warlike destruction, that we could crumple up the Russian Empire by blockading her ports, and sealing hermetically that semi-barbarous country, so that she could have no communication whatever with the rest of the civilized world. That was what I said. Well; but why do I rate so low the power of the Russian empire? It is because every thing we have seen in the progress of that country proves that she is comparatively weak, particularly beyond her own frontiers. I don't say within her own borders, because she has shown in the case of Napoleon that if you go there you will find but an inhospitable reception. But all history proves that Russia is a very weak country when she attempts to carry on a war beyond her own border."

And as an illustration of the moral power which can be exercised by a great people, without any imposing demonstration of force, he said: "There is that boy-Emperor of Austria, who has been wasting his time ever since he came to the throne in reviewing troops, surrounded by his gilded state and a staff of fifty or sixty generals. If a single frigate were sent by that plain man in a black suit of clothes in the Capitol at Washington to Trieste, with a hostile message, would not that boy-emperor's heart be in his very jack-boots when he received it?"

Ere turning to an entirely new aspect of Cobden's career, when he found his own and the nation's opinion receding farther and farther from, instead of advancing nearer and nearer to, each other, we present, as the conclusion of this chapter, a pen-and-ink sketch of him, about this time, limned by Harriet Beecher Stowe in her "Sunny Memories."

"*Monday morning, May* 23. We went to breakfast at Mr. Cobden's. Mr. C. is a man of slender frame, rather under than over the middle size, with great ease of manner and flexibility of movement, and the most frank, fascinating smile. His appearance is a sufficient account of his popularity, for he seems to be one of those men who carry about them an atmosphere of vivacity and

social exhilaration.   We had a very pleasant and
social time, discussing and comparing things in
England and America.   Mr. Cobden assured us
that he had curious calls from Americans sometimes.   Once an editor of a small village paper
called, who had been making a tour through the
rural districts of England.   He said that he had
asked some mowers how they were prospering.
They answered, 'We ain't prosperin', we're hay-
in'.'   Said Cobden, 'I told the man, Now don't
you go home and publish that in your paper;
but he did nevertheless, and sent me over the paper with the story in it.' . . . . The conversation turned on the question of the cultivation
of cotton by free labor.   The importance of this
great measure was fully appreciated by Mr. Cobden, as it must be by all.   The difficulties to be
overcome in establishing the movement were no
less clearly seen and ably pointed out.   On the
whole, the comparison of views was not only interesting in a high degree, but to us, at least, evidently profitable.   We ventured to augur favorably to the cause from the indications of that interview."

CHAPTER X.

PERIOD OF THE CRIMEAN WAR.

MR. COBDEN acted with his usual courageousness in the matter of the Crimean War. He differed with the mass of the English people about the policy of entering upon it, and he, with equal manliness and clearness, put the grounds of his difference from the prevailing opinion upon record. These grounds we regard it our incumbent duty to reproduce in his own words, or, at all events, in a summary of the few speeches and the pamphlet which proceeded from him during the war, which shall be as faithful a transcript as the necessary brevity of our undertaking allows, of Cobden's *ipsissima verba ;* and we also incorporate with our narrative a citation from Mr. Kinglake's great work, "The Invasion of the Crimea," as representing with tolerable fairness the objective view—the view held by Mr. Cobden's fellow-citizens — of his conduct at this very important crisis of the nation's history. We must, however, interpose the *caveat* — which, indeed, the previous context of our remarks would almost make unnecessary — that we can not agree with Mr. Kinglake in his estimate of the doings of Mr.

Cobden and the Peace Society in the peaceful years anterior to the outbreak of the war between Nicholas and the Porte, in which England, with other Western Powers, found herself involved. Mr. Kinglake thus nervously, and, on the whole, impartially writes of Cobden and Bright at this era:

" Mr. Cobden and Mr. Bright were members of the House of Commons. Both had the gift of a manly, strenuous eloquence; and their diction, being founded upon English lore rather than upon shreds of weak Latin, went straight to the mind of their hearers. Of these men, the one could persuade, the other could attack; and, indeed, Mr. Bright's oratory was singularly well qualified for preventing an erroneous acquiescence in the policy of the day; for, besides that he was honest and fearless—besides that, with a ringing voice, he had all the clearness and force which resulted from his great natural gifts, as well as from his one-sided method of thinking, he had the advantage of generally being able to speak in a state of sincere anger. In former years, while their minds were disciplined by the almost mathematical exactness of the reasonings on which they relied, and when they were acting in concert with the shrewd traders of the North who had a very plain object in view, these two orators had shown with what a strength, with what a masterly skill, with what patience, with what a high courage they could carry a great scientific truth through the storms of politics. They had shown that they could arouse and govern the assenting thousands who listened to them with delight— that they could bend the House of Commons— that they could press their creed upon a prime minister, and put upon his mind so hard a stress that, after a while, he felt it to be a torture and a violence to his reason to have to make stand against them. Nay, more; each of these two gifted men had proved that they could go bravely into the midst of angry opponents — could show them their fallacies one by one — destroy their favorite theories before their very faces, and triumphantly argue them down. Now these two men were honestly devoted to the cause of peace. They honestly believed that the impending war with Russia was a needless war. There was no stain upon their names. How came it that they sank, and were able to make no good stand for the cause they loved so well?

"The answer is simple.

"Upon the question of peace or war (the very question upon which, more than any other, a man might well desire to make his counsels tell) these two gifted men had forfeited their hold upon the ear of the country. They had forfeited it by their former want of moderation. It was not by any intemperate words upon the question of this war with Russia that they had shut themselves out from the counsels of the nation; but in former years they had adopted and put forward, in their strenuous way, some of the more extravagant doctrines of the Peace Party. In times when no war was in question, they had run down the practice of war in terms so broad and indiscriminate, that they were understood to commit themselves to a disapproval of all wars not strictly defensive, and to decline to treat as defensive those wars which, although not waged against an actual invader of the queen's dominions, might still be undertaken by England in the performance of a European duty, or for the purpose of checking the undue ascendency of another power. Of course the knowledge that they held doctrines of this wide sort disqualified them from arguing with any effect against the war then impending. A man can not have weight as the opponent of any particular war if he is one who is known to be against almost all war. It is vain for him to offer to be moderate for the nonce, and to propose to argue the question in a way which his hearers will recognize. In vain he declares that for the sake of argument he will lay aside his own broad principles, and mimic the reasoning of his hearers. Practical men know that his mind is under the sway of an antecedent determination, which dispenses him from the more narrow but more important inquiry in which they are engaged. They will not give ear to one who is striving to lay down the conclusions which ought, as he says, to follow other men's principles. He who altogether abjures the juice of the grape can not usefully criticise the vintage of any particular year; and a man who is the steady adversary of wars in general, upon broad and paramount grounds, will never be regarded as a sound judge of the question whether any particular war is wicked or righteous, nor whether it is foolish or wise. . . . . Lord Aberdeen and Mr. Gladstone consenting to remain members of a war-going government, and Mr. Cobden and Mr. Bright being disqualified for useful debate by the nature of their opinions, no stand could be made."

Ere proceeding to transcribe Mr. Cobden's own explanation and justification of his conduct in this matter, it will serve more than one useful purpose to make brief reference to a speech delivered by him at a public meeting held at the London Tavern in the early part of 1850, upon the then proposed Russian Loan. The sentiments then and there delivered by him make it abundantly clear that it was no sordid regard for Russia, as a growing, if not already a great, market for our manufactures, that induced him to offer pacific counsels. And in this speech he showed himself to be a sincere and sympathetic friend of distressed nationalities. It acquits him of the charge—one by no means unfrequently brought against him—of being indifferent and callous to the progress, the struggles, and the wounds of liberty abroad. He was, it must be admitted, extremely cautious as to the overt expression of sympathy for the oppressed peoples of the world ; for he had seen how outspoken utterances from Englishmen had fed such unfortunates with vain hopes of English interference, and thereby incited them to the prolongation of struggles whose failure made their woes more grievous than before, and entailed upon them additional exasperated strokes of dynastic vengeance. The remark may seem ungenerous, but we confess that we think it, to say the very least, very questionable whether the Circassians are not to-day in a worse plight than if Mr. Urquhart had never been born, or employed at the Turkish Embassy—whether Lord Dudley Stuart's speeches and Earl Russell's dispatches may not have heightened the agonies of the Poles—and whether the vengeance of the Czar and the Kaiser upon the Magyars might not have been less severe had some one else than Lord Palmerston been at the Foreign Office in 1848. Be that as it may, Mr. Cobden's course in such matters was at least logical, and not only self-consistent, but perfectly compatible with the warmest love of liberty, the most intense hatred of enthroned wrong, and the tenderest commiseration for enthralled right. We the more gladly make reference to, and citation from this speech, inasmuch as it was one of his happiest. It belonged to that class of his speeches—a class which formed a large constituent part of them—which may be termed chatty and conversational; in which he put himself at once and peculiarly at ease with his audience, and equally discarded oratorical effort and rhetorical verbiage.

The plea upon which the Czar came to the English money market for five and a half millions sterling was that it was wanted for the completion of the railroad from St. Petersburg to Moscow. Mr. Cobden commenced by flatly declaring that this was untrue—and that he had been at St. Petersburg three years previously, and seen that the rolling stock of the railway was complete. Even if he did want it for making a railway, it was ridiculous to suppose that he would need it all in six months, which was the condition of his request. "Here are railway calls from one railway alone at the rate of nearly one million a month, and that in a country where, up to the month of March, no work can be done in the way of forming embankments, and consequently this money is wanted for the purpose of being expended in excavating and embanking in the months of April, May, June, and July. I really pity the mendicant Czar who is obliged to come to us with such a story."

But why, he went on to say, should he, as a Free Trader (he had been asked), interfere with such a loan? "Why not let people lend their money in the dearest market, and borrow it in the cheapest?"   He answered, "I have no objection to people investing their money, if they like to do so; but I claim the right as a Free Trader, in a free country, to meet my fellow-citizens in a public assembly like the present, to try and warn the unwary against being deceived by those agents and money-mongers in the city of London who will endeavor to palm off their bad securities on us if they can."

"But," he went on, "apart altogether from these grounds of its inherent immorality and insecurity, I stand here as a citizen of this country, and as a citizen of the world, to denounce the whole character of this transaction as injurious to the best interests of society.   I will take first the politico-economical view of the question, because it is supposed that on this question I am particularly weak in that direction.   Now I take my stand on one of the strongest grounds in stating that Adam Smith and other great authorities on political economy are opposed to the very principle of such loans.   What is this money wanted for?   It is to be wasted.   It is to go to defray the expense of maintaining standing armies, or to pay the expenses of the atrocious war in Hungary.   Then what does it amount to?   It is so much capital abstracted from England and handed over to another country to be wasted, thereby abstracting from the labor population of this country the means by which it is employed and by which it is to live. I say that every loan advanced to a foreign power to be expended in armaments, or for carrying on war with other countries, is as much money wasted and destroyed for all the purposes of reproduction as if it were carried out into the Atlantic and there sunk in the sea. And I make no distinction whether the interest be paid or not—for if it be paid by the Emperor of Russia, it is not paid out of the proceeds of the capital lent—it is not paid out of the capital itself being invested in reproductive employment; but it is extorted from the labor, the industry, and the wretchedness of his people, to pay for the interest of that capital which has not only not been employed in reproductive labor, or even thrown into the ocean, but far worse, in abstracting industry, in devastating fair and fruitful lands, and in suppressing freedom."

The following sentences were uttered by a man who more than once during his public life was called a Philo-Russian!

"Now what is this money wanted for? Simply and solely to make up the arrears caused by the exhaustion of the Hungarian War. I am not in the habit of boasting at public meetings of what I may have done on former occasions, but if I were a boaster I should exult that the assertions I made on this spot in June last, and which have been subjected to so much sarcasm from

foes and friends—I should, I say, feel some exultation that this poverty-stricken Czar has been
obliged to come forward and verify every word
I then said. What has become of the two millions we were told the Emperor has subscribed
to the Austrian loan? What has become of the
£500,000 he was going to advance to the Pope,
or the half million he was going to bestow in his
generosity on the Grand-Duke of Tuscany? Oh,
he ought to pay his scribes well in Western Europe who have told so many lies for him! He
ought to pay them well, seeing that they have
been subjected to this full refutation of all they
said in his behalf at the hands of the Czar himself.
If I had been employed to write up the wealth,
power, and riches of a man who six months after
was obliged to come before the citizens of London and sign his name to such a humiliating
document as this imperial ukase, I should expect
to be exceedingly well paid for the loss of character I had sustained. Well, I stand here, to repeat the very words I uttered twice on this platform at times when few would believe me. I say
that the Russian government in matters of finance
has been for years — successfully, until now the
bubble has burst—the most gigantic imposture
in Europe. I use the words, as I hope I do every word I say at a public meeting, advisedly. I
have used them before, and, after due investiga-
tion, I came here to repeat them. I say that this

money is wanted for the purpose of sustaining the ambition, the sanguinary brutality of a despot, who has all the tastes of Peter the Great, and all the lust of conquest of Louis XIV., without the genius of the one or the wealth of the other; and who would apply their principles to a great part of Europe, forgetting that this is the nineteenth instead of the seventeenth century; while utterly wanting not merely the ability which would enable him to play such a part in history, but even the pecuniary means of enjoying the tastes he possesses."

We conclude our quotations from this speech, so memorable and important an incident in the life of Cobden, with the following anecdotal paragraph.

"I came down this morning from the West-end of the town in an omnibus, sitting opposite to a gentleman. As we were riding along, he looked out of the window and saw a placard with the words 'Great meeting on the Russian Loan.' He said to me, 'Mr. Cobden is going to have a meeting, I believe.' 'Yes,' said I, 'I believe he is.' 'It's very odd,' he observed, 'that he should presume to dictate to capitalists as to how they should lay out their money.' 'Well,' said I, 'if he attempts to dictate, it is rather hard. But I suppose he allows you to do as you like.' 'But,' said he, 'he holds public meetings to denounce the loan; yet I should not wonder if he would be

very glad himself to have £20,000 of it.'   I said,
'Have you taken any yourself?'   He replied, 'I
have—£50,000, and I intend to pay it all up.'   I
then said to him, 'Would you like to leave that
property to your children?   'No,' he said, 'I
don't intend to keep it more than two years at
the outside, and I hope to get a couple per cent.
profit upon it.'   Now it is with that view that
that gentleman is going to pay up his calls—that
is, if he thinks of doing so.   That is not the ordinary case; they generally pay up one call, and
then sell the stock at any profit which they can
get upon it; and the loss of holding these securities — I said it before, and I repeat it now — the
loss falls upon individuals who were totally un-
connected with the taking of the loan — trades-
men retired from business, widows and orphans,
trustees and others who invest money in what
they regard as a permanent security, in order to
obtain the interest upon it.   Well, now, I declare
most solemnly, after looking into this subject of
Russia as I have done for the last eighteen years,
that I would not give five-and-twenty pounds per
cent. for the Russian Five per Cent. stock, which
is being dealt in to-day by the Bulls and Bears at
107.   I would not take £100 at that price for permanent investment, and with the view of leaving
it as a part of the dependence of my children."

Mr. Cobden spoke in the House of Commons
very seldom while we were " drifting into" and

carrying on the Crimean War. He entered his dignified protest against the revival of the war spirit in the land—the sentiment expressed in Tennyson's pæan of joy that "the long, long canker of peace was over and done." He did so, and then he retired, refusing to cumber the ground and increase the irritation by farther invectives and cautions. He deliberately expressed his views in 1853 and the spring of 1854, ere the country was quite committed, and subsequently he only addressed the House when terms of peace were under consideration, and when, accordingly, his voice might do good. The chief arguments and considerations adduced by him were these. He held that the integrity and independence of the Turkish Empire, as a maxim of policy, had become an empty phrase and nothing more. The Turks were intruders in Europe; their home was Asia; the progress of events had demonstrated that a Mohammedan power could not be maintained in Europe. The independence of a country that could not maintain itself could not be upheld; and if he himself were a Rayah, a Christian subject of the Porte, he should say, "Give me any Christian government rather than a Mohammedan." We should hereafter have to address our minds to the question what we were going to do with Turkey, for we must not think that we could keep Turkey as it was. He ridiculed the notion of going to war for tariffs, the futility of which policy experience had proved, and he contended that the importance of the trade with Turkey had been overrated. He maintained that all our commerce in the Black Sea was owing to Russian encroachment. As for the talk of a Russian army invading England (which prevailed in some quarters), why, Russia could not move her forces across her own frontier without a loan.

As the war became more imminent, he pointed out that the whole difference between Russia and the other powers consisted in this—that the Great Powers wished that the grievances of the Christians should be redressed by themselves, acting together and in concert, and not by Russia; and for this despicable ground of quarrel Europe was to be deluged in blood. Undoubtedly the Christian population were looking for ameliorations, whether from Russia or elsewhere. He said it was chimerical to expect any substantial change in their treatment, which could only be brought about by an abandonment by the Mussulmans of their religious principles and an abrogation of the law of the Koran. Replying to the arguments upon the other side, founded upon the comparative value of the trade with Russia and Turkey, he declared the Russian trade to be of thrice the importance to this country of the Turkish. If there was real danger, as Lord John Russell had alleged, " to all mankind," those nearest the danger ought to be the first to meet it. If we were

going really to fight for the Turks, let us fight
with our navy, and not send a miserable 20,000
troops to the Danube. [This was, of course, before
the expedition to the Crimea was resolved on.]

Early in 1855 there was a great debate on a
motion of Mr. Milner Gibson for an address to the
crown to this general effect, that the propositions
made by Russia at the Vienna Conference contained the germs of reasonable pacification, and,
therefore, that the negotiations should be vigorously and hopefully pursued. All the great representatives of all parties spoke. Mr. Layard also
had given notice of a motion denouncing the in-
efficiency of the administration, and of the conduct of the war, and its source—the favoritism of
our governmental system. This already compo-
site discussion was still farther complicated by a
resolution of Mr. Disraeli, pledging the House to
"dissatisfaction with the ambiguous language and
uncertain conduct of her majesty's government
in reference to the great question of peace and
war." The House, night after night, debated together the rival propositions. Disraeli made one
of his most sarcastic orations, his chief victim being Lord John Russell, who had just made so woe-
ful a failure at Vienna as a diplomatist. After
his denunciation of "diplomatic subterfuge and
ministerial trifling," Sir Francis Baring interposed
an amendment, expressing continued confidence
in the government. Sir William Heathcote intro-

duced still another amendment, expressing more definitely than Sir Francis Baring's a strong desire for the return of peace, which gained the valuable adherence of Mr. Gladstone, who was not then a minister. After speeches from many members of secondary weight, and from Sir William Molesworth, Sir Bulwer Lytton, Lords Palmerston, Stanley, and Lord John Russell, Mr. Cobden, having adjourned the debate at a late hour, resumed it on the following day. Sir William Molesworth had urged the rejection of the Russian proposals, and the prolongation of the war. Mr. Cobden especially reproached him for desertion of his old principles. He maintained that the slight difference between Russia and ourselves on the famous "Third Point" was not sufficient to justify the continuance of the war. Russia, he said, had been denounced for bad faith, and yet we were prepared to join with her in guaranteeing the governments of Wallachia and Moldavia, and the protocols reposing trust in Russia to this extent were signed by the very cabinet ministers who had so denounced her. He pungently contrasted Lord John Russell's polite conduct abroad with his violent speeches at home. The language and conduct of the ministers were one continued seesaw, changed from time to time to suit the press and the feeling out of doors. He taunted ministers with the deferment of the promised and boasted co-operation of Austria; but his main point was the natural development of Russia in the Black Sea, which he showed had been more rapid than even that of the United States of America. It was, he admitted, only a youthful barbarian developing himself into something better; but, while he continued with no other neighbor than the decaying and unimproving Turkish Empire, all the powers on earth could not take from Russia her preponderance in these regions, which was inherent in the nature of things.

Our readers will have vividly brought back to their recollections the height and fervor of the war spirit of 1855, and the utter hopelessness of Mr. Cobden affecting it in the slightest degree, by the perusal of these few lines of Lord Palmerston's speech in reply to Mr. Cobden. He was speaking of the so-called "peace-at-any-price men."

"With peace in their mouths, they have, nevertheless, had war in their hearts; and their speeches are full of passion, vituperation, and abuse, and delivered in a manner which shows that angry passions strive for mastery within them. I must say, judging from their speeches, their manner, and their language, that they would do much better for leaders of a party for war at all hazards, instead of a party for peace at any cost. Mr. Cobden did at last tell us that he would fight —no, not that he would fight—but he said that there was something for which the country must fight; and he added, that if Portsmouth were menaced — he said nothing about the Isle of Wight—he would go into the hospital. Well, there are many people in this country who think that the party to which the honorable gentleman belongs would do well to go immediately into a hospital of a different kind from that which the honorable gentleman meant, and which I shall not mention." It is not much to be wondered at that Cobden, Liberal politician though he was, should mournfully say, a few weeks after, "I look back with regret on the vote which I gave on the motion which changed Lord Derby's government. I regret the result of that motion, for it has cost the country a hundred millions of treasure, and between twenty and thirty thousand good lives."

A still more astounding indication of the fevered spirit at this period prevailing is furnished by this incident. Mr. Joseph Sturge, like the other Peace Society leaders, manfully avowed among his neighbors and elsewhere his opinion of the war; and he received more than his own share of obloquy. A placard was put up in Birmingham entitled "War and Dear Bread," showing how war enhanced the price of food, and it was popularly attributed to Mr. Sturge. He received a number of anonymous letters accusing him of hoarding large quantities of grain to enhance its value, and threatening vengeance. Mr. Sturge wrote a general reply to his anonymous correspondents, and had it inserted in the local newspapers, stating, " If the writer of this letter will give me his name, I shall be glad to meet him and his friends, and if they can point out how *I* can lower the price of bread to the public, I shall rejoice to join them in any legitimate means to carry their plan into effect."   When Mr. Cobden heard of this, he wrote to his friend : " It is amusing to see the mad vagaries of the persons who charge *you*, of all men, with being the cause of dear bread !   It reminds me of what occurred after the great French War had produced its natural consequences — dear bread and want of employment—when the London mob in the neighborhood of Spitalfields directed their vengeance against the Quakers as being the authors of their misery — the Quakers having been, be it remembered, almost the only people who steadily opposed the said clamorous mob.   You will see this referred to incidentally in the first volume of the *Life of William Allen*, p. 50."

It was some consolation to Cobden to have the sustenance and support of such men as Sturge. Sturge wrote of Cobden to an American friend in February, 1855, "John Bright and Richard Cobden are acting a noble part in resisting the war mania ; and the fearful carnage it occasions, as well as the increasing sufferings among our poor, are bringing many over to their opinion who were a short time ago in favor of the war."

Cobden said no more on the subject in the House of Commons, but brought out, early in 1856, his pamphlet, " What Next — and Next?" in which he besought the country to consider whither it was tending, and asked it to endeavor to realize its own ends and objects in the war, and to consider both the cost and the likelihood of their attainment. He pointed out the fact that a country like England is peculiarly unsuited for aggressive military enterprises: " A manufacturing community is, of all others, the least adapted for great aggressive military enterprises like that in which we have embarked. In defending themselves at their own doors, such an industrial organization might afford greater facilities, probably, than any other state of society; for the men, being already marshaled (so to speak) in regiments and companies, and known to their employers, the resources of the capitalists and the services of the laborers might be brought, with precision and economy, into instant and most extended co-operation. We read that Jack of Newbury (the Gott of his day) led a hundred of his clothiers, at his own expense, to Flodden Field; and if the spirit of patriotism were roused by the attack of a foreign enemy, I have no doubt we should see our great manufacturing capitalists competing for the honor of equipping and paying the greatest number of men until our shores were freed from the presence of the invader. But I am obliged to presuppose an invasion of our own territory before assuming that all ranks would be roused to take a part in the struggle."

At last, to Cobden's great delight, peace came. In one respect, the Peace of Paris contained a great triumph for him, although it came to him most unexpectedly. In the treaty was incorporated the very Arbitration clause for which he had been battling, and for which he had been so jeered in the English House of Commons. When the peace was proclaimed, a deputation waited upon Lord Palmerston on the subject, but he raised all sorts of objections, and held out no hope. Mr. Henry Richard then suggested that a journey should be undertaken to the very fountain-head, Paris, where the plenipotentiaries sat. He met with but scant encouragement. His friends (including Cobden, it would appear) dissuaded him from the bootless errand. Sturge, however, said, "Thou art right; if no one else will go with thee, I will; and I am prepared to go, not only to Paris, but, if necessary, to Berlin, Vienna, Turin, and even to St. Petersburg, should there be time, and see if we can't get access to the various sovereigns whose plenipotentiaries are sitting at Paris." They went, visited Lord Clarendon, and obtained the promise: "I will do what I can to bring the matter before the Congress." He did so, was supported by the French and Prussian plenipotentiaries, and when the treaty was promulgated it was found to contain this clause:

"The plenipotentiaries do not hesitate to express, in the name of their governments, the wish that states between which any serious misunderstanding may arise should, before appealing to arms, have recourse, so far as circumstances might allow, to the good offices of a friendly power. The plenipotentiaries hope that the governments not represented at the Congress will unite in the sentiment which has inspired the wish recorded in this protocol."

"This happy innovation," as Lord Clarendon termed it, consoled Cobden in some degree for his heartache of the last two years. In the very House which had laughed at his proposal only a short time ago, Mr. Gladstone spoke eloquently of this protocol as "a powerful engine on behalf of civilization and humanity," and said it "asserted the supremacy of reason, of justice, humanity, and religion." Even Lord Derby accorded "endless honor" to the diplomatists for adopting it, and Lord Malmesbury talked of its "importance to civilization and to the security of the peace of Europe," because "it recognizes and establishes the immortal truth that time, by giving place for reason to operate, is as much a preventive as a healer of hostilities." This was by no means the smallest of Cobden's triumphs.

CHAPTER XI.

THE CHINA WAR, AND THE FRENCH TREATY.

MR. COBDEN's whole career may be characterized as having displayed the continuous and consistent pursuit, exposition, and advocacy of a few fixed and definite ideas. These, at an early period, fairly took possession of his whole mind and being, and may be said to have saturated, and permeated to its extremities, his very existence. The remaining portion of Mr. Cobden's life may be greatly compressed, for it consisted of no more than the renewed and continued application of those principles of his policy which we have already, in an expository manner, propounded, to the public questions which arose, either in our domestic or our foreign policy, from year to year. Cobden's views and tenets remained the same —quite unchanged. The form of their application might vary somewhat, as the conditions and contingencies to which they were applied varied. New forms of illustration might be introduced, as when he made himself master of the whole novel and intricate questions of shore fortifications and naval armaments, as they came before the public with all the modern experience of the

Crimean and American Wars, the bombardments
of Sebastopol and Charleston, and the encounter
of the *Monitor* and *Merrimac*. He brought to
the debates on these and cognate themes a practical knowledge which put him quite on an equal
footing with our great administrators, soldiers,
contractors, and engineers. He held his own
with, or against, the Palmerstons, Burgoynes,
Ellenboroughs, Lairds, and Petos. In addition
to showing, on general grounds, the needlessness
and folly of excessive international defenses and
armaments, and the certainty of their causing
wanton acerbity and ill blood, he descended into
the more technical arena of the minor premiss
disputed, and showed that, even if his general
views on national armaments were erroneous—
ceding that major point for the sake of argument
—nevertheless, the nation was acting unadvisedly
about the *kinds* of armament it selected. Even
if great and costly armaments were necessary, it
was foolish, he said, to go on building experimental ships, or casting experimental guns, in the
uncertain and transitionary states of the sciences
of artillery and ship-building, and to construct
great stone fortifications, when positive evidence
had shown their fragility, and negative evidence
the superior impregnability of hastily-constructed
earthen ramparts. In such minor and special
particulars, the course of his argumentation and
the line of his advocacy were modified and af-

fected by circumstances; but his principles remained the same: he only reiterated them. A brief and compendious summary, therefore, of his leading utterances during the last eight years of his Parliamentary career will be sufficient for our purpose.

Cobden differed from the majority of his fellow-countrymen about the Chinese War of 1857, as he had dissented from the popular voice and will about the Russian War of 1854. News had been received in England of a serious misunderstanding with the Chinese authorities. A small vessel called the *Arrow*, of a peculiar local form and rig designated by the term *lorcha*, and which had a British colonial register, lay in the Canton River a little below the foreign factories. No notice having been given to the British consul, she was boarded by a party of the Chinese marine. Her flag was torn down, and her whole Chinese crew carried away on a charge of piracy. The British consul, Mr. Parkes, remonstrated, but without avail. The Chinese commissioner, Yeh, gave no heed to his representations. Nor was our superior diplomatic agent, Sir John Bowring, a whit more successful. The matter was then relegated to the admiral of the station, Sir Michael Seymour, to obtain satisfaction for the alleged wrong to the English flag. His menaces proving equally unavailing, and more than one term of grace having expired, he proceeded to overt acts, and reduced fort after fort along the river sides, destroyed a fleet of junks, shelled the city, and demolished its chief public buildings.

The English government at once avowed, justified, and declared their intention to stand by the acts of their officials. At home, opinions were divided about the justice and propriety of the procedure. Lord Derby took the sense of the House of Lords on a motion adverse to the ministers, and Mr. Cobden adopted the same course in the Lower House. The keenest debates occurred in both assemblies; and the division list in the Commons' House was by far the largest which had been known in its history. Mr. Cobden's resolution was couched in these terms: "That this House has heard with concern of the conflicts which have occurred between the British and Chinese authorities in the Canton River; and without expressing an opinion as to the extent to which the government of China may have afforded this country cause of complaint respecting the non-fulfillment of the treaty of 1842, this House considers that the papers which have been laid upon the table fail to establish satisfactory grounds for the violent measures resorted to at Canton in the late affair of the *Arrow;* and that a select committee be appointed to inquire into the state of our commercial relations with China." Without going too definitely, he said, into what we had actually done, he contented himself with inquiring, Would we have done what we had done if we had been dealing with a strong power, and not a weak one? He contrasted the conduct of the British authorities at Hong Kong with that which we would have pursued had the government we dealt with been at Washington, and the transaction had taken place at Charleston. He conscientiously believed that there had been a preconceived design to pick a quarrel with the Chinese, for which the whole world would cry shame upon us. The papers he looked upon as a garbled record of trumpery complaints against the Chinese. He quoted extracts from travelers testifying to the civility and inoffensive habits of the Chinese, and reminded his auditors of the haughty demeanor and inflexible bearing toward the natives of other countries which Englishmen carried abroad with them. As for the clause in the treaty enforcing the admission of Englishmen into Canton, he expressed his opinion that it was a chimera. It was not worth fighting for. If this part of the treaty could be at once enforced, it would be of no use to us. He also specially blamed the conduct of Sir John Bowring, alleging that he had acted directly contrary to his instructions.

The Tories and the Peelites united with the Radicals in support of the motion. Among the speakers adverse to the government were Sir E. B. Lytton, Messrs. Warren and Whiteside, Sir

James Graham, Dr. Phillimore, Sir Frederick Thesiger, Sidney Herbert, Roundell Palmer, Mr. Henley, Messrs. Gladstone and Disraeli. In a word, the whole character and oratorical power of the House, save what was possessed by ministerialist office-holders and office-seekers, ranged themselves under Cobden's leadership. He carried his motion by a majority of sixteen. And this was the more wonderful, that, in the House of Lords, where Toryism so largely preponderated, Lord Derby's similar motion was defeated by a majority of thirty-six.

Lord Palmerston had the option of dissolution or resignation. He chose the former, and went to the country. The natural excitement of the public mind, coupled with the zealous advocacy of the ministerial prints, and the bellicose speeches of the ministerial candidates, added to those other less obvious, but perhaps more operative influences which ministers can always bring to bear at election times, produced from the people an entirely different verdict from that which had been delivered by their parliamentary representatives. The name of Palmerston became the rallying cry at every hustings. In fact, the populace ignored even the consideration of the absolute merits of the question under dispute. They simply remembered that Palmerston had carried them through the Crimean War, when other politicians had wavered and shrunk from its responsibility. They recounted with admiration his versatile and varied talents, his *bonhommie* and gallantry against opposition, and the wondrous energy with which he combated and spurned the natural influences of growing old age. The results were a marvelous ministerial majority, and the exclusion from Parliament of Cobden, Bright, Milner Gibson, Layard, J. W. Fox, Miall, and not a few of the Peelites of the second grade. Cobden had not again sought the suffrages of his West Riding constituents. He had discovered in the course of his canvass that he had no chance of success there; and when he made the discovery, he rebuked them for their tergiversation from their old principles, at Leeds and other great towns of the Riding, in tones as distinguished by manly outspokenness as they were marked by the entire absence of all querulousness or personal chagrin. He then solicited the suffrages of the citizens of Huddersfield; but the voters there gave the preference to a thorough-going ministerialist, and Cobden was for the first time since he first entered Parliament without a seat.

A beautiful incident occurred during this stirring period of our recent history. While the general election was going on, Bright, who had shortly before been compelled by ill health to leave the country, was still so ill as to be unable to return to conduct his own canvass at Manchester; Cobden and others of his friends discharged that task for him. Shortly after the common rejection of Cobden and Bright, the former attended and addressed a meeting at Manchester. In the course of his speech he alluded to his friend's defeat, and dwelt upon the fact that the Manchester men had rejected the man of whom they had been so proud, at a time when he was afflicted, and necessarily absent by reason of ill health. He became at once deeply affected—the more so, that Mr. Bright's health was believed to be still most dangerously affected. He could not go on; his eyes filled with tears, and for a time he was reduced to absolute silence. This eloquence was felt to be far more expressive than the most fluent sentences of objurgation or reproach. When one recollects such an occasion of the expression of ardent personal attachment between the two men, or such as was reciprocally shown by Bright in speaking of the House of Commons the day after Cobden died, how strongly is one reminded of the forcible but indisputable expression of Cicero—" Nulla potest amicitia nisi inter bonos !"

For rather more than two years Mr. Cobden was absent from Parliament. Part of his leisure was filled up by a somewhat lengthened tour in the United States. It was not long after his rejection by the voters for the West Riding and the electors of Huddersfield ere the country began to be rather ashamed of its conduct in rejecting so many of its best men in its China War fervor. Among others of the discarded who were from time to time reseated was Mr. Cobden, who was ultimately returned by Rochdale while he was yet absent from England. In Cobden's absence, Mr. Milner Gibson had avenged the cause of conscientious Radicalism upon Lord Palmerston by defeating him upon the Conspiracy to Murder Bill. The Tories had come in; Mr. Disraeli had introduced his Reform Bill; it was opposed by Lord John Russell on the ground of the meagreness of its provisions; the Radicals formed a coalition with the Whigs at the famous Willis's Rooms meeting. Their combined forces defeated the government. Lord Palmerston was once more sent for, and he announced his determination to reserve certain seats in his cabinet and ministry for the leaders of advanced Liberalism. Meanwhile, Mr. Cobden had not yet returned to England. It was only on his arrival at Liverpool that he learned from a deputation of gentlemen who went off and boarded the steamer by which he voyaged that the premier had designated him to the appropriate office of President of the Board of Trade. On his landing, he accepted a solicitation to address a meeting; and although, as he himself said, his head was yet swimming from the effects of sea-sickness, he delivered a speech cogent and telling, clear and perspicuous, which might well have been supposed to have been the result of much study and elaborate preparation.

Mr. Cobden determined not to accept the proffer-
ed post. He called upon Lord Palmerston at
·Cambridge House, and frankly told his lordship
he could not serve under him. It was understood that when Palmerston remonstrated and advised reconsideration, Cobden rejoined that he
had always regarded him as a most dangerous
minister for England, and that his views still remained the same; and that he felt that he would
be doing violence to his own sense of duty and
destroying his character for consistency if he attempted to act with a minister to whom he had
all along been opposed.

While Cobden was out of Parliament, the question of the short war with Persia, and the more
important incident of the Indian Mutiny, had been
the chief subjects of discussion. Although he
was precluded from uttering his views in St.
Stephen's Hall, he let it be known through other
channels that he strongly condemned the chronic
misgovernment which produced the revolt of our
Sepoys, and that he supported—as might indeed
have been supposed — that " clemency" of Lord
Canning after the disturbances were virtually
quelled which was the subject of such angry ani-
madversion within and without the walls of Parliament.

In 1853, the periodical date of the legal expiry
of the East India Company's twenty years' charter had come round. It was strongly urged that

their tenure of power should not be renewed for the same term, but that a year or two's time should be allowed to intervene for full consideration of all the aspects of the question of India and her relation to the home government ere legislation for a lengthened period was again effected. In the debates of that year Cobden had taken a leading part, so that his opinions were fairly before the nation in advance of the crash of the mutiny. He described the Court of Directors as a mere sham, a screen behind which that governing body, which was real, and therefore ought to be responsible, might shelter itself. The two were respectively the John Doe and the Richard Roe, shams of law which had been then lately done away with. India should be governed in the same way as the colonies, so that English public opinion should reach it—this was its only chance. Thus only could wars and annexations be got rid of. The President of the Board of Control might actually annex China, if he so chose, against the will of the Secret Committee. As to patronage, he desired appointments to be given to the natives, which the Board of Directors were certain never to do. As to the fiscal question, he said it was impossible to separate the fate of Indian and English finances. He showed that there had been an aggregate defalcation in twenty years amounting to twenty-eight millions. And those who had proved that they could not take stock in a way which, in the case of the humblest trader, would satisfy a bankruptcy judge, were not fit to administer the finances of India. As the territory had increased, so had the debt; and Sattara, Scinde, and the Punjaub were all admittedly governed at a loss.

We need hardly say how thoroughly the startling shock of the mutiny brought home these and such considerations to the minds of the English people. The result was the final quietus of the Company, except as a body of guaranteed fundholders, and the fair assumption by England of those responsibilities of the government of its most magnificent dependency, which Cobden six years previously had warmly urged her to undertake.

Cobden, though declining to be an actual member of the second administration of Lord Palmerston, offered no objection to act as its representative in the negotiation of the French Treaty. In the latter case, he avoided—what he could not have escaped in the former—all general complicity with the plans and policy of ministers. The French Treaty of Commerce thus, or somewhat thus, came about. Strong in his denunciation as he had been of the frequent panics of French invasion of England, the idea gradually grew upon him that by far the most effectual method of rendering their recurrence most unlikely, if not quite impossible, was to cement new ties of commercial intercourse connecting the two countries, between which for ages there had been a most foolish and mutually injurious rivalry of prohibitory tariffs, and thus establish the strongest interests on both sides of the Channel against the outbreak of war. He had frequently talked over this idea with other illustrious Free Traders, notably with such men as Chevalier and Bright; and Bright publicly expounded it and urged its adoption, in a speech delivered shortly after the formation of the ministry in 1859. Chevalier, when he read this speech, wrote to Cobden, stating his belief that the time was now ripe for the completion of the idea which had formed so frequent a subject of their mutual converse and their dearest hopes. Chevalier said he believed the co-operation of the Emperor was certain. This was a great encouragement to Cobden, and he resolved fairly to set about the task. He communicated his plans to Mr. Bright, and the two proceeded to Hawarden Castle, the seat of Sir Stephen Glyn, a relative of Mr. Gladstone, and whom the latter gentleman was then visiting. Mr. Gladstone accorded at once his warmest approval. Cobden then waited upon the premier, who also sanctioned the enterprise, and Mr. Cobden at once proceeded to Paris to commence the execution of his difficult but glorious task. Into the details of the long-protracted negotiation; the enormous obstacles of prejudice to be overcome in France, the most

Protectionist of European lands; the devoted
loyalty of the Emperor from first to last; the effectual aid received from such Frenchmen as
Bastiat, Chevalier, and the Minister Rouher; the
valuable support afforded to Mr. Cobden by his
appointed coadjutor in the business of negotiation, Mr. Mallet, of the Foreign Office—into these,
and the other most interesting minute particulars
of the transaction, it is impossible to enter; and
it would be writing a history rather than a biography, and therefore quite stretching and exceeding the prescribed purpose of our plan, were we
to enter upon the pleasing digression of nar-
rating, even in brief, the story of the hard fight
against the treaty in the English House of Commons, and the gallant stand made for it, and its
absent negotiator, by Palmerston, Gladstone, Milner Gibson, and many others equally worthy of
honor. Nor shall we enter at length into what
all the newspapers, Board of Trade Returns,
Financial Statements, and general experience of
the trading and industrial portion of the nation,
have each and all equally brought to light since
it was carried; the astounding impetus to, and
yearly increasing development of the international commercial transactions of the two lands which
it has affected and blessed.

The broad features of the treaty may be compressed within a very few lines. On the 1st of
October, 1861, France was to reduce duties and

take away prohibitions on British productions
mentioned, on which there was to be an *ad va-
lorem* duty of 30 per cent. There was a provision that the maximum of 30 per cent. should,
after the lapse of three years, be reduced to a
maximum of 25 per cent. England engaged, with
a limited power of exception, to abolish immediately and totally all duties on manufactured
goods, to reduce the duty on brandy from 15*s.* to
8*s.* 2*d.*, on wine from 5*s.* 10*d.* to 3*s.*, with power
reserved to increase the duty on wine if we raised
our own excise duties on spirits. England engaged to charge upon French articles subject to
excise the same duties which the manufacturer
would be put to in consequence of the changes.
Considerable reductions, both present and pro-
spective, were made upon the charges levied on
English iron, coal and coke, carried into France.
The treaty to be in force for ten years.

Probably in the whole history of diplomacy, if
we consider the disturbing views and opposing
interests to be conciliated or vanquished, the in-
tricacy of detail of negotiation, the novelty of
the proposal, the brief period in which all was
accomplished, no one feat so wondrous was ever
achieved by one man. Cobden lived to see all
the morose vaticinations both of French and English opponents disappointed. He lived to hear
from his antagonists their own candid confessions
of their error; and the French manufacturing

classes, who were five years before the most Protectionist body in Europe, not only vied with the English people in their expressions of sorrow at Cobden's death, but it was a common saying of English travelers to France, in the spring and early summer of 1865, that they actually believed that the mourning for Cobden occupied more deeply the French bosom than the English, or was at least more loudly demonstrated by the subjects of the Corsican than the subjects of the Guelph.

From the English ministry Cobden had not to wait for so tardy (though, when it came, so pleasing) an acknowledgment. Mr. Gladstone said in his place in Parliament: "With regard to Mr. Cobden, speaking as I do at a time when every angry passion has passed away, I can not help expressing our obligations to him for the labor he has, at no small personal sacrifice, bestowed upon a measure which he, not the least among the apostles of Free Trade, believes to be one of the most memorable triumphs Free Trade has ever achieved. Rare is the privilege of any man who, having fourteen years ago rendered to his country one signal and splendid service, now again, within the same brief span of life, decorated neither by rank nor title, bearing no mark to distinguish him from the people whom he loves, has been permitted to perform a great and memorable service to his sovereign and to his country."

After the successful completion of the French treaty, Lord Palmerston, on the part of her majesty, offered to Mr. Cobden a baronetcy and a place in the Privy Council. Cobden declined both the hereditary rank and the personal honor. He chose to be content without ordinary and official reward; and perhaps this was just as well. The titles and rewards of office have often been misapplied; have been, with almost equal frequency, conferred for discreditable and detrimental as for beneficial services; have been as often bestowed upon the favorites of kings and the instruments of their tyranny—sometimes even of their vices—as upon the benefactors of the people and the promoters of their best interests. Cobden doubtless felt this, and feeling this, one may acquit him of any cynical independence and affected republican simplicity in his respectful refusal of the honors offered him by his sovereign and her appointed minister.

Posterity, rather than ourselves, will be able to estimate the full amount of the benefit to England and humanity constituted by and contained in the French treaty. Only when a century shall have passed without any war between England and France shall the livers in that blessed epoch be able to contrast with sufficient emphasis with the five previous centuries of English history the peaceful era inaugurated by Cobden's far-seeing scheme for withdrawing the risks of war and multiplying the bonds of peace; for, from the time of the earliest Plantagenets up to the days of our own immediate fathers, it seemed all through to be almost an axiom of English policy and feeling that we should be always picking quarrels with, or accepting challenges from, the sons of Gaul, and dealing upon them our doughtiest blows. Every ship we launched, every gun we cast, every regiment we embodied, were launched, cast, and embodied that they might be used against France. In more olden times, our youth were trained in the use of cross and long bows, all with a view to the fights at Cressy, Agincourt, Orleans, and Calais. On France all our bellicose energies were concentrated. Literally, up till Tudor times she was the only Continental power we ever fought with; and since the days of the Armada, even, we fought with her more frequently, and at far greater cost, than with all other powers combined. Kings like James, and ministers like Walpole, were unpopular because they would not war with France; and at the end of his unloved reign, the Second George gained, to his own surprise, great popularity, and Chatham's popularity became more excessive than ever minister's had been before, or has been since, when they committed the nation to war with France. Maria Theresa was the darling of our nation, and even the rough and unloveable Frederick the Great became the same when they entered into alliance with us—or, rather, we with them, for the quarrels were theirs—against France. All this is altered now, and, we trust in Heaven, shall ever so remain. To Cobden, more than any other man, will posterity admit that it is indebted for the holy and propitious change.

P

CHAPTER XII.

LAST YEARS IN PARLIAMENT.

DURING the whole of 1861 Cobden spoke only once in the House of Commons. This was in behalf of the repeal of the Paper Duty, the last remnant of those taxes on knowledge which he had assailed all his life. Just when he started as a public man—but as yet not known beyond the confines of his own borough and neighborhood— he had taken a respectable share in the agitation for the reduction of newspaper stamps and the charge for postage. He lived to see the very last artificial shackle on intelligence and its dissemination removed, and he helped in no mean degree to its removal. His speech, which was on the Budget of this year generally, was but a brief one. He had been away from the House, doing better work for England in Paris than he could in London. "I am not," said he, "going to trouble the committee at any great length. I am not sufficiently conversant with your recent debates to do so."

The following compliment to the newspaper press of this country, as a literate profession, is certainly one of which it may well be proud :

" You are aiming at preventing the Chancellor of the Exchequer from continuing in a course which he has not the merit of originating. I can not give him the credit for the least originality, nor can he be accused of precipitation. He is only going in the path which every government must follow, whether it be called Whig or Tory. Is it for the advantage of honorable gentlemen opposite that they should place themselves in this position? If you succeed by a majority in overturning the government and coming in yourself, you must instantly adopt the very policy which you are opposing in opposition. There is no alternative. The principle rooted in the public mind of England is to remove those barriers which impede the progress of commerce and. manufactures, so as to give the chance of employment for a growing and an increasing population. You yourselves have the greatest interest in promoting that policy, and in nothing more than the repeal of the paper duty, by which you offer the advantage of employment to a class superior to those affected by any other article subject to the Excise Duty; for bear in mind that there is no article which gives employment to the same educated class of men as paper. If I were a young man just fresh from college, with nothing in the world but a good education, there is nothing I should look for with so much interest as making perfectly free the press of this country, by removing all the taxes which tend to render dear and scarce literary productions. What should I want? I should want employment for my pen. Is it not an advantage to rising educated young men that more editors, more contributors, more short-hand writers should be required ?"

On the 3d of June, 1862, Mr. Stansfeld proposed in the House of Commons a resolution to the effect "that the national expenditure is capable of reduction, without compromising the safety, the independence, or the legitimate influence of the country." This was a great field-night in the House. Several amendments had been put upon the paper, two or three of them more or less friendly to the government, and one — that of Mr. Walpole — was supposed to be designed to raise the direct issue of "no confidence.". It was believed that once more a conjoint Tory-Radical attack was to be made upon ministers, and that there was a chance of Lord Derby and his party coming in. There was a crowded House, an unusually disorderly preliminary debate — an overture, as it were, to the great performance which was to follow—and altogether a very great deal of interest, bustle, and excitement. Mr. Cobden spoke just before the close of the discussion, making no allusion whatever to its supposed party aspects, which, indeed, turned out not to exist in the intentions of the movers either of the motion or of any of the amendments. The general gist of Mr Cobden's speech may be given very briefly. After a severe reply to Mr. Horsman, whom he rightly accused of the most callous carelessness to the real welfare of the nation so long as the armaments were kept in their inflated state, he undertook to deal with the stale and nauseating plea that our expenditure was kept up on account of the necessity to protect ourselves against France. Why should we not endeavor to produce quiet and peace in a cheaper way? We were in alliance with France; why could not Lord Palmerston, or somebody else— he (Mr. Cobden) would undertake to do it—take the matter in hand, and talk over the question of the iron vessels? He said the consequences would be perfectly disastrous unless the government would address themselves to the task of retrenchment, and to the relations of this country with France. Thus felicitously and pertinently did he demonstrate from contemporary events the truth that it is reserved resources of material wealth, and not huge armaments eating into the vitals of nations, that are the real conquerors when the push comes.

"Look at what is going on beyond the Atlantic. Every body has complained that America was very overbearing in her foreign policy. Very well; but bear in mind that America was never well armed. She had but fourteen or fifteen thousand soldiers; she never would have a fleet; she has not had a line-of-battle ship in commission for the last ten years — certainly not more than one. If, then, America played the bully without arms, what was it that impressed her will upon the rest of the world?   Undoubtedly it was that you gave her credit for having vast resources behind her, which were not unnecessarily displayed in a state of armed defiance.   Well, what has been the result of the present deplorable war in America? You have seen that country manifesting a power such as I have no hesitation in saying no nation of the same population ever manifested in the same time.   No country in Europe, possessing 20,000,000 of people, could put forth the might, could show the resonrces in men, money, and equipments that the Federal States of America have done during the last twelve months.   Taking the whole country together, about thirty millions of people have kept nearly 1,000,000 men in arms; and they have, upon the whole, been equipped and supplied as no other army ever was before.   Why was that?   Simply because the Americans had not exhausted themselves previously by high taxation.   They were a prosperous people.   Their wages and profits were high, because their taxation was low; and as they were earning twice as much as the people of Europe earned when the war broke out, they had only to restrict themselves to one half of their usual enjoyments, and they found means of carrying on the war. That, I think, is a doctrine that applies to us as well as to the Americans, and I deny the doctrine that a nation increases its power, and is better prepared for carrying on war, because it always maintains a large war establishment in time of peace."

One of the last great and telling speeches delivered by Cobden in the House of Commons was on the proposal of the government to expend, within a given number of years, a sum of £20,000,000 on the additional fortifications of our dock-yards and arsenals. In this he undertook to prove that the alarmist government statements about the strength of the French navy were "entirely fallacious and delusive." This proposition he supported by a long array of figures. "In the whole of the past five years I defy any one to show an instance in which the noble lord (Palmerston) has advocated an increase of our naval armament in reference to any other country but France. We have heard from him the word 'invasion' a dozen times within the last few years. Now, for a prime minister to talk about this country being invaded by a friendly power, without one fact to justify a suspicion of it — on the contrary, when the navy of that government is less than at any former time —is to commit this country to an attitude toward that neighboring power that no minister ought to give it with the levity of indiscretion that has marked the noble lord's course on the subject."

Some passages from the conclusion of this spirited address we quote without any farther comment than to call the reader's attention to the confirmation, falling from Mr. Cobden's own lips, of a statement made by us in a previous page, about the matured and moderate character of his views on the question of Peace.

"There is no question in this House as to defending the country against a foreign enemy. It would be a piece of supreme impertinence in me, or in any other man, to lay claim to an exclusive interest or regard for the security of the country against a foreign enemy, and I hold the man to be a charlatan who sets up a claim to popularity because he holds the honor and safety of the country in higher estimation than I do. That is not the question here, where every man has an equal interest in the safety of the country. We may take different views — as we are entitled to do—as to the best modes of fortifying and permanently defending the country. Some think we can not do better than appeal for armaments and fortifications in addition to our existing resources in times of peace, notwithstanding the weight of taxation under which the country is struggling; while others, like myself, may think, with Sir Robert Peel, that you can not defend every part of your coast and colonies, and that, in attempting to do so, you run a greater risk of danger to the country than you would incur by husbanding the resources which you are now expending upon armaments, so as to have them at call in time of emergency. That is my view. Let no one presume or dare to say that he has more regard for the safety of the country than I have. They may try to create imaginary dangers, and to take credit for guarding against them; but give us a real danger, show us that our navy is not equal to our defense, that a neighbor is clandestinely and unduly trying to change the proportion which its force should bear to that of this mercantile people living in an island, *and then I would willingly vote* £100,000,000 *of money to protect our country against attack.* But in saying this I claim no merit. I do not set myself up as a great patriot, for there is nobody here but would put his hand in his pocket and spend his whole fortune rather than have this island defiled by the foot of an enemy. . . . . .

"Our wealth, commerce, and manufactures grow out of the skilled labor of men working in metals. There is not one of those men who, in case of our being assailed by a foreign power, would not in three weeks or a fortnight be available with their hard hands and thoughtful brains for the manufacture of instruments of war. That is not an industry that requires you at every step to multiply your armed men. What has given us our Armstrongs, our Whitworths, our Fairbairns? The industry of the country, in which they are mainly occupied. It has been sometimes made

a reproach against me and my friends, the Free
Traders, that we would leave the country defenseless.   I say, if you have multiplied the means
of defense—if you can build three times as many
steamers in the same time as other countries, and
if you have that threefold force of mechanics to
which my honorable friend has spoken, to whom
do you owe that but to the men who, by con-
tending for the true principles of commerce, have
created a demand for the labor of an increased
number of artisans in this country?   Go to Plym-
outh or to Woolwich, and look at the names of
the inventors of the tools for making fire-arms,
and shot and shell.   They bear the names of men
in Birmingham, in Manchester, and in Leeds—
men nearly all connected for the last twenty years
with the extension of our commerce, which has
thus contributed to the increase of the strength
of the country, by calling forth its genius and
skill.   I resist the attempt which has been made
to show that I am not a promoter of the strength,
the power, and the greatness of this country, or
that I, or any of those who act with me, are, or
have been indifferent to, or ignorant of, what con-
stitutes the real strength and greatness of the
country."

The last occasion on which Mr. Cobden addressed the House of Commons was on July 22d,
1864, when he made an unusually lengthened and
elaborate speech, bristling with facts and figures,

and permeated by sound practical experience and common sense. The occasion was his moving a series of resolutions condemnatory of the great extension of the government manufacturing establishments. He cited as an authority Burke, who, in a speech delivered in 1780, "laid down, in language which it is impossible to surpass, the reasons why the government should not manufacture its own supplies, but should depend on the competition of individual manufacturers." He said the negligence of Parliament and the Treasury had become so great, and the departments had taken upon themselves such an immense increase of manufacture, that they laughed at the idea of Parliament superintending the details of the administration. Indeed, Mr. Cobden himself objected to Parliament undertaking such intricate functions. He thought the House could interfere with great advantage in prescribing the principles on which the executive government could be carried on, but beyond that he held it to be impossible for the Legislature to interfere with advantage in the details of the administration of the country. And he said that in the early years of his experience in Parliament, when Sir Robert Peel was prime minister, he would have resented the appointment of the Parliamentary committees of inquiry into the details of administration which now prevail as tantamount to votes of want of confidence. Sir Robert would have said, if such a committee had been proposed in his time, and while he held the reins of power, " If you think the administration is not satisfactorily conducted by me, then you must find somebody else to undertake it."

To give some idea of the rapidity of the rate at which the government had become manufacturers, Mr. Cobden reminded the House that up till the close of the Crimean War the British government had never cast a cannon, or made a shot or shell. And when it was determined to cast 68-pounders at Woolwich, the proprietors of the Low Moor works, who had previously supplied the government, and who not only took selected qualities of their own iron—which is the best—but used coal of a peculiar kind, fresh from the earth, to smelt it, would not sell pig iron to the Woolwich establishment. The result was that, having got the machinery for casting the guns, there was no iron fit to cast. They had to go into the market and buy the ordinary kind of pig iron, and, as a consequence, the guns were pronounced rotten and were never used. He then told the exactly similar and parallel story of the government and Whitworth and Armstrong guns. He dwelt with great scornful glee upon the naïveté with which the leading men at Woolwich came before the committee appointed by the House, and tried to show that they were producing the guns cheaper than at Elswick, Sir

William Armstrong's factory; forgetting that the two were one and the same concern, Sir William's works being as much a government establishment as those at Woolwich! for they were both started by the government with the nation's capital.

Then he went on to small-arms, and showed that exactly the same course had been pursued in this field. Till the close of the Crimean War the government did not manufacture a single rifle. They were furnished by private contractors, and spoken of in the highest terms by the Sebastopol Committee of 1855, while the medical, commissariat, and other departments were unflinchingly condemned. But the government got an idea into their heads that at some moment of dire necessity, when they were in great need of rifles, there might be a strike among some class of the workmen who manufacture their various parts; the more so, as if only the maker of the lock struck, it would stop the manufacture and delivery of the whole rifle. This was quite true, and the natural remedy was that they should give orders to capitalists, who would set up machinery for manufacturing the whole musket. But government could not be made to comprehend a thing so obvious as this, and erected an enormous manufactory for the construction of rifled small-arms at Enfield, and they actually sent to America to procure the requisite machinery. And now all had gone for nothing; for the superiority of

the Lancaster and Whitworth to the Enfield rifles
had been acknowledged.

After entering into similar and more extended
details, Cobden said he found that he never could
make the conductors of these government establishments understand that the capital they had to
deal with was really money. For how should it
be real money to them? It cost them nothing.
Whether they made a profit or a loss, they never
made their way into the *Gazette*. To them money
was a myth; to the tax-payers, however, it was a
reality. You never could make the gentlemen at
the head of the departments understand that they
must pay interest for capital, rent for land, as well
as allow for depreciation of plant and machinery.
He said the manner in which the government officials chuckled over the supposed greater cheapness of their results in comparison with those of
the private manufacturer always reminded him of
the story of two gipsies who sold brooms. One
said to the other, "I can't conceive how you can
afford to sell your brooms cheaper than I do, for
I steal all my materials." "Ah!" says the other,
"but I steal my brooms ready made."

Then he went on in the same vein of serious
depreciation, enlivened by the keenest irony, to
the army tailoring department, jocularly terming
Lord De Grey and Ripon "the most extensive
tailor in the world." · Then he went from land to
sea, propounding once more his oft-reiterated

views as to the folly of large expenditure for
ships in the present transitionary state of naval
architecture and the science of gunnery. The last
words of this remarkable speech—and the last
words uttered by Cobden in the House of Commons—were these. They are a sacred legacy left
to the nation he loved so well.

"I know of nothing so calculated some day to
produce a democratic revolution as for the proud
and combative people of this country to find
themselves, in this vital matter of their defense,
sacrificed through the mismanagement and neg-
lect of the class to whom, with so much liberal-
ity, they have confided the care and future desti-
nies of the country. You have brought this upon
yourselves by undertaking to be producers and
manufacturers. I advise you in future to place
yourselves entirely in dependence upon the private manufacturing resources of the country. If
you want gunpowder, artillery, small-arms, or the
hulls of ships of war, let it be known that you
depend upon the private enterprise of the country, and you will get them. At all events, you
will absolve yourselves from the responsibility of
undertaking to do things which you are not competent to do, and you will be entitled to say to
the British people, 'Our fortunes as a government
and nation are indissolubly united, and we will
rise or fall, flourish or fade together, according to
the energy, enterprise, and ability of the great

body of the manufacturing and industrious community.' "

Speaking with strict accuracy, these were not absolutely Cobden's last words in the House. For subsequently, in the same debate, he, curiously enough, interrupted a speaker with the characteristic ejaculation, "It is ridiculous to compare times of peace and war."

The last time Mr. Cobden appeared before and addressed a public audience was on the 23d of November, 1864, when he gave to his Rochdale constituents his customary annual review of the session, and his general opinions upon current questions of public policy and affairs. Mr. Bright was also to have been present, but was compelled to be absent in consequence of the recent death of a son of great promise. Mr. Cobden could well sympathize with a calamity like this, and the opening sentences of his long, comprehensive, and spirited address contained most kind and touching references to the affliction of his friend and constituent. Mr. Cobden never uttered a more thoroughly characteristic address than this. All his leading qualities were displayed in it. Merely premising that the chief topics which he touched were the Schleswig-Holstein debates of the preceding session; the collapse of the doctrine of intervention to which these debates had testified; the course of the American War; the questions in dispute between Federals and Confederates, and the financial condition and prosperity of England, we proceed to cull a few of the more representative passages of this speech. We make no attempt at summarizing, commenting on, or furnishing connecting links to our citations. We shall best do our duty to the original and to our readers by letting Mr. Cobden speak for himself. And to read these words solemnizes one, for they were the last he uttered in public.

"Let me tell the solid, substantial, manufacturing, and commercial capitalists of the country that this is not a very honorable position to be left in. They allowed the government to go on and commit them in encouraging a small power to fight with a big one. It was very much like a man backing a little fellow for a prize-fight, drawing him to the scratch where his toe is to come to, telling him how to plant himself, superintending his training, and assuming responsibility for all he does, and then, as soon as blows are exchanged, running off. That is the position in which we were left by what happened last session in regard to Schleswig-Holstein, and we are caricatured in every country of Europe. I myself saw German and French caricatures immediately afterward. There was a French one representing Britannia with a cotton night-cap on. I recollect a picture of the British lion running off as hard as he could, pursued by a hare. That is not a satisfactory state of things, because I maintain that to a cer-

Q

tain extent we deserve all this — that is, we deserve it unless we show that we did not run away merely because it did not suit us to fight, but that we intended to adopt a new principle in our foreign policy, and that other countries must not expect us to fight except for our own business. . .

"It is said we must form our armaments upon a new scale, in order to prevent France from swallowing up Germany. Now I think that if France were to perform such a feat as that, she would suffer so terribly from indigestion after swallowing these forty millions of uncomfortable Teutons, I think she would be an object of pity rather than terror ever afterward. Well, now, really it is surprising to hear men aspiring to be statesmen come and talk exactly as if they had taken passages from *Baron Munchausen or Gulliver's Travels.* How can we say that we have made any great progress if such sentiments can be paraded on the banks of the Roche, and what must we expect to hear from the agricultural districts in the neighborhood of Midhurst?. . . . . My right honorable friend [Mr. Bouverie, M.P., in a then recently delivered speech], when he advocates the carrying out of the sentimental policy, carries us as far back as the time of Queen Elizabeth, and says that she was a sovereign who did what was right, and true, and just, and in the interest of Protestantism, all over the Continent of Europe. . . . . . When I read Motley's 'History of the Dutch Republic'—when I read this history of the rise of the Netherlands, and when I see that struggling community with their whole country desolated by Spanish bigotry, and every town lit up daily by the fires of persecutors—when I look at what passes when the envoys come to Queen Elizabeth to ask her aid, how she is huckstering for money while they are talking of religion, I declare, with all my doctrines of non-intervention, I am almost ashamed of Queen Bess, and of her grasping ministers, Burleigh and Walsingham. . .

" What did the Americans do when they declared their independence in 1776? They put forth a declaration of grievances, and at the present time no Englishman can doubt that they were justified in separating from the mother country. . . . . But why is there [by the Confederate leaders] no such declaration? Because they have but the grievance they want to consolidate, perpetuate, and extend—slavery; but they can not do it. . . . . What do they say? Leave us alone; all we want is to be left alone. That is the reason why the conservative governments of Europe, and so large a portion of the upper classes in England, have consented to back the insurrection. Now how would they feel if Essex and Kent, having been beaten on the subject of the Corn Laws, had chosen to set up Kent and Essex, and East Anglia right across the Thames, as the Secessionists have sought to attempt to cut off Louisiana from the

mouth of the Mississippi, and if they had said,
' We want to be left alone'—why, can any government be carried on if a section of the people, when
they are beaten at the poll at a peaceful election,
be allowed to secede? I ask where is the conservatism among the governing class of the country?
I come to the conclusion that, after all, there is
more conservatism among the democracy. . . . . .

"If I were a rich man, I would endow a profess-
or's chair at Oxford and Cambridge to instruct
the undergraduates of those universities in American history. I would undertake to say, and I
speak advisedly, that I will take any undergradu-
ate now at Oxford or Cambridge, and ask him to
put his finger on Chicago, and I will undertake to
say that he does not go within a thousand miles
of it. . . . . When I was at Athens I sallied out
one summer morning to seek the famous river, the
Ilissus, and after walking some hundred yards or
so up what appeared to be the bed of a mountain
torrent, I came upon a number of Athenian laun-
dresses, and I found that they had dammed up
this famous classical stream, and were using every
drop of its water for their own sanitary purposes.
Why, then, should not these young gentlemen,
who know all about the geography of the Ilissus,
know also something about the geography of the
Mississippi? . . . . To bring up young men from
college with no knowledge of the country in which
the great drama of modern politics and national

life is now being worked out, who are ignorant
of a country like America, but who, whether it
be for good or for evil, must exercise more influence in this country than any other class—to bring
up the young destitute of such knowledge, and
to place them in responsible positions in the government, is, I say, imperiling its best interests;
and earnest remonstrances ought to be made
against such a state of education by every public
man who values, in the slightest degree, the future welfare of his country."

Probably, had Mr. Cobden himself been able to
penetrate the inscrutable future—had he uttered
his speech with the consciousness that it was to
be his last—he would have made selection of these
following sentences which concluded this admirable and now sacred oration:

"Do you suppose it possible, when the knowledge of the principles of political economy has elevated the working classes, and when that eleva-
tion is continually progressing, that you can permanently exclude the whole mass of them from
the franchise? It is their interest to set about
solving the problem, and, to prevent any danger,
they ought to do so without farther delay."

CHAPTER XIII.

LAST DAYS, AND DEATH.

For the last three or four years of Mr. Cobden's life he suffered from an asthmatic affection, and was recommended, as each succeeding winter came round, to repair to a milder climate. But he disregarded the injunctions, and preferred to remain in his own country home, now rendered more sacred to him by the burial in the grave-yard which was ere long to receive his own remains, of his only son. The younger Cobden, a youth of great promise, died in Germany, where he was pursuing his education. His remains were conveyed to England, and buried in West Lavington church-yard, a spot of remarkable beauty, and which Mr. Cobden selected as the burial-place of himself and his family, in preference to the cemetery of his own parish of Heyshot.

Mr. Cobden's daily life at Dunford was of a remarkably beautiful and touching character. All his life a being of strong affections and singular gentleness, these lovely traits became more striking as he grew older, being mellowed and intensified by his great domestic sorrow. He was surrounded by the memories of his family, and the

WEST LAVINGTON CHURCH.

outward records of the existence of its successive generations. His own house, though rebuilt and modernized when the estate was purchased for him, contained intact a part (we believe, his mother's bedroom) of the old house in which he had been born, and which had been occupied by his father and grandfather. The Cobden family had been owners of freehold land in Sussex from the time of Henry VIII., if not from an earlier date. Close by stands an ancient building called Cranmoore farm-house, now divided into two laborer's dwellings, which local tradition says was the residence of the Cobden family — then, as more recently, yeomen freeholders—a century and a half ago. An old yew-tree, the sole occupant of his lawn, had witnessed the advent and the passing away of many successive generations of the Cobdens, and a fine pine wood upon his estate, which formed his favorite walk, and under whose shade Mr. Bright and he discussed, only three weeks before his death, the policy of the nation, must have been nearly coeval with the association of the Cobdens with Dunford. In fine weather, his favorite ride was to Cowdray, the old residence of the Montagues; or he would drive through the pleasant parishes of Heyshot and Graffham to the family seat of the Bishop of Oxford, with whom he was accustomed to stay once or twice every year.

Mr. Cobden's hospitality at Dunford was very

conspicuous, and its objects were as various as its
kindness was undoubted. The cosmopolitan character of his mind and heart, and the world-wide
beneficial range of his efforts, were fairly reflected in the national varieties of his guests, who
came to him from all parts of the earth. With
them he would sit up far into the night, never
weary of conversing, and — a rarer faculty — as
ready to listen as to talk. His large correspondence cemented and enlarged the circle of his
friends. He was a prodigious letter-writer, and
a very admirable one. A note of his in answer to
the most ordinary query was sure to be exhaust-
ive, and in most cases was suggestive, going into
new and additional aspects of the question to that
submitted, and furnishing his querist with considerable more of information or counsel than had
been solicited. He would frequently rise at six
in the morning to write letters; and, says a most
appreciative biographer in a morning newspaper,
to whom we have gratefully to acknowledge our
indebtedness for many of the facts and traits we
reproduce in this chapter, " If the sky was cloudy
or the weather broken, he would often write till
post-time, perhaps alternating his epistolary duties with reading some favorite author, a recrea-
tion of which he was never weary. Like a famous
ancient, he was never less idle than when he was
idle, nor ever less alone than when he was alone."

We have frequently denied ourselves the gratification, and our readers the advantage, of presenting characteristic passages from Mr. Cobden's letters at various stages of the pleasant labor whose results are embodied in the preceding pages. Ere taking leave of our subject we present two of Mr. Cobden's letters; one of them, we believe, the very last he penned. They are both on most important themes, and on subjects whose interest is any thing but evanescent. They may justly be considered legacies of opinion left behind him, bequeathed in the interests of his mourning compatriots and his fellow-men. The former of the two is upon the progress of the American War, and on certain of the questions of policy incidental to its development. It was addressed by Mr. Cobden to the American minister at Copenhagen, and runs as follows. It will be observed that all the surmises contained in the second paragraph turned out absolute predictions, and were being literally realized just about the time of Mr. Cobden's death.

"Midhurst, February 5.

"My dear Friend,—I duly received your letter of the 12th of December. Ever since I have been an invalid, not having left the house for more than two months. I was imprudent in going at so late a season to address my constituents in the North, and was unfortunate in being obliged to speak not only for myself, but for Mr.

Bright, who was prevented from being present by the death of his son. But I am better now, though not well enough to be at my post at the opening of the session. I must wait for finer weather.

"I congratulate you on the course which events have taken in your country during the last few months. It seems to me that there are unmistakable signs of exhaustion in the Confederacy, and it would not be rash to predict now that the famous 'ninety days' will witness very decisive events in the progress of the war. Jefferson Davis rules in Richmond, but the Federal armies control his dominions. I hold a theory that in these times, when armies require vast appliances of mechanical resources, and when they are so much larger than in olden days, it is impossible to carry on war without the base of large cities. If the sea-ports be taken and Lee be obliged to evacuate Richmond, there will not be a town left in the Confederacy with 20,000 white inhabitants. It will be impossible to maintain permanently large armies in the interior of the slave states, amid scattered plantations and unpaved villages. You can not, in such circumstances, concentrate the means of subsistence or furnish the necessary equipment for an army. I expect, therefore, to see the loss of the large towns lead to a dispersion of the Southern armies. I have sometimes speculated on what course Lee will take if obliged to abandon his position at Richmond. I have my doubts whether he will continue the struggle beyond the borders of his native state. However, all these are speculations which a few months will dispose of. I pray Heaven we may soon see the termination of this terrible war.

"I observe what you say about Confederate agents having found encouragement in Europe. I can easily believe this. If the South caves in there will be a fierce resentment felt by the leaders toward those potentates or ministers in Europe who have deluded them to their ruin, and I should not be surprised if we were to hear some secrets disclosed, in consequence, of an interesting kind. Democracy has discovered how very few friends it has in Europe among the ruling class. It has at the same time discovered its own strength, and, what is more, this has been discovered by the aristocracies and absolutisms of the Old World, so that I think you are more safe than ever against the risks of intervention from this side of the Atlantic. Besides, you must not forget that the working class of England, who will not be always without direct political power, have, in spite of their sufferings and the attempt made to mislead them, adhered nobly to the cause of civilization and freedom.

"You will have a task sufficient to employ all your energies at home in bringing your finances into order. There is a dreadful want of capacity

at your head in questions of political economy;
you seem now to be in the same state of ignorance
as that from which we began to emerge forty
years ago. The labors of Huskisson, Peel, and
Gladstone seem never to have been heard of by
Messrs. —— and Co. Depend on it that as there
is no royal road to learning, so there is no republican path to prosperity. You must follow the
beaten track of experience. Debt is debt, whether
on the west or east of the Atlantic, and it can be
paid only by prudence and economy, and a wise
distribution of its burdens. . . . .

" Yours, very truly,
"R. Cobden.

"Hon. B. R. Wood."

The other letter, the last which proceeded from
his pen, was addressed to Mr. Potter, now Mr.
Cobden's successor as M.P. for Rochdale, and is
on the subject of a scheme recently propounded
by Mr. John Stuart Mill, which, with all respect
for its author, we can not help agreeing with Mr.
Cobden in regarding as somewhat cumbrous and
crotchety, for the better parliamentary representation of minorities. The letter seems to us an
admirable specimen of the clearness and sagacity
of Mr. Cobden's intellect. It did not reach its
destination by post, but was found in his desk
after his death.

"London, 23 Suffolk Street, Pall Mall,
March 22, 1865.

"My dear Potter,—I return Mill's letter. Every thing from him is entitled to respectful consideration. But I confess, after the best attention to the proposed representation of minorities which I can give it, I am so stupid as to fail to see its merits. He speaks of 50,000 electors having to elect five members, and that 30,000 may elect them all, and to obviate this he would give the 20,000 minority two votes. But I would give only one vote to each elector, and one representative to each constituency. Instead of the 50,000 returning five in a lump, I would have five constituencies of 10,000, each returning one member. Thus, if the metropolis, for example, were entitled, with a fair distribution of electoral power, to 40 votes, I would divide it into 40 districts or wards, each to return one member; and in this way every class and every variety of opinion would have a chance of a fair representation. Belgravia, Marylebone, St. James, St. Giles, Whitechapel, Spitalfields, etc., would each and all have their members. I don't know any better plan for giving all opinions a chance of being heard; and, after all, it is opinions that are to be represented. If the minority have a faith that their opinions, and not those of the majority, are the true ones, then let them agitate and discuss until their principles are in the ascendant. This is the motive for political action and the healthy agitation of public life. I do not like to recognize the necessity of dealing with the working-men as a class in an extension of the franchise. The small shop-keeper and the artisan of the towns are socially on a level. The subject is, however, too large for a sheet of note-paper. Believe me, yours very truly,

"R. COBDEN."

The writer to whom we have already acknowledged our indebtedness thus completes his notice of Mr. Cobden at Dunford during the last period of his life:

"The public are able to judge of his powers as a letter-writer, of that clearness and vigor of style which shone as brightly in his briefest notes as in his most studied speeches; but only a comparative few of the outer world have had the opportunity of being fascinated by his conversation, or feeling the magic spell which he cast around him in private life. He had also the rare faculty of abstracting himself from surrounding objects, and, like some other great men, of sleeping at will—perhaps the secret of that recuperative power with which so fragile a man must have been endowed. While his life at Midhurst was simplicity itself, its chief beauty consisted in the ample fulfillment of every positive duty. His affection for his cattle, and for animals of all kinds, was great, but his love for his fellow-creatures was correspondingly greater. He never forgot that he was not only a member for a distant constituency, and a statesman with high public functions to perform, but that he was a parishioner of Heyshot, and that serious obligations devolved upon him within a stone's-throw from his own door. At first he occupied the whole of his land himself, but latterly he let a portion of it to the oldest farmer in the parish — a veteran who mourns for him as for a son; and as he had spent a great deal of money in improving and draining it, no one could place him in the same category with a certain class of the Irish landlords. He took a deep and abiding interest in the welfare of the poor people in the neighborhood. Occasionally, when his health admitted, he would call upon them; and he was constantly inquiring about them individually in his house. Many of these poor persons have, at various times, been objects of his generous and discriminating bounty — all regarded him as a friend to whom they could with confidence appeal in the hour of need. He took a deep personal interest in the establishment of a school, and was extremely anxious to establish penny readings for the benefit of the villagers, and to get lecturers from a distance who would talk to them on improving subjects. As a member of the Church of England, he was as devoted to the cause of religion as he was to the interests of education. No man could take more pride in

R

his parish church, or exhibit a more laudable desire to make it the focus and centre of a blessed,
heaven-inspired influence. So long as he was able,
he never failed to be present at divine worship
beneath the venerable roof of Heyshot Church,
in the precincts of which his brother was buried;
and only the extreme inclemency of winter prevented him from participating in its pure and
elevating ritual. He took a chief part in originating the improvements in the church, and the
music has more recently been the object of his
pious care. An old poet has said,

> " 'Only the actions of the just
>   Smell sweet and blossom in the dust.'

This applies with singular relevance to Mr. Cobden; and, indeed, as the present writer can af-
firm, only those who have conversed with the men
and women who were familiar with his every-
day life, who were privileged to know or to discover the good things he did openly, or, as he
best loved, in secret, can form an adequate idea
of the pure and noble life of this Christian statesman and philanthropist."

Although not obtrusively communicative on
public occasions of points of religious faith, Mr.
Cobden was a really religious man. A frequent
remark of his was, "You have no hold of any one
who has no religious faith."

The physical prostration which succeeded the

great speech at Rochdale, in November, 1864, once more reminded Mr. Cobden how dangerous it was for him to appear in public during an English winter. He never got the better of it, and declared his intention not to resume his parliamentary duties until spring had fairly set in. In January, 1865, Mr. Gladstone wrote to Mr. Cobden, offering for his acceptance the important post of chairman of the Board of Audit, a permanent office, with a salary of £2000 a year. Mr. Cobden at once declined the flattering and lucrative office, alleging that he could not subject himself to the pain and annoyance which his discharge of the duties must involve, of witnessing, and appearing to sanction without any power to prevent, the scandalous and unnecessary waste of public money.

Mr. Cobden was inspired with the deepest interest in the progress in Parliament of the discussions on the alleged necessity of undertaking large works of defense in the Canadas. Early in March he invited Mr. Bright to come to Dunford, that they might converse together on the subject, and concert the best means of impressing their common views on the government and the nation. He asked Mr. Bright to come into Sussex, because he did not deem it advisable to go to London in the very inclement and wintry weather which still prevailed. In the course of his converse with Mr. Bright, he referred to the fact that his son was buried in Lavington church-yard, and stated that there too, when God took him, he would be buried. As the Canada debates progressed, he was seized with an irresistible desire to go up to London, and expound his opinions in Parliament. He came to town on the twenty-first of March, one of the bitterest days of the very severe and trying spring of the year. Immediately on his arrival at his house in Suffolk Street he was seized with an attack of asthma. A week after, he had sufficiently recovered to be able to see some of his friends. But on the afternoon of Wednesday, the twenty-ninth, the attack returned with renewed severity. For a day the attentions of his medical attendant, and the sedulous care of his wife and second daughter, prevented at least an increase in the malignity of the disorder, and hopes of his recovery were entertained. On Friday, the last day of March, the symptoms were considered unfavorable, but on Saturday morning he was again held to be a little better; but as the day proceeded he grew decidedly worse, the disease becoming developed into what is termed congestive asthma, and being farther complicated by an attack of bronchitis. In the course of the day he made his will, appointing as his executors Mrs. Cobden and the Messrs. Thomasson, senior and junior, of Bolton. He also dictated a letter to Mr. Bazley, M.P., Mr. Henry Ashworth, of Bolton, and Mr. John Slagg, of Manchester, with reference to certain funds which these gentlemen held in trust for his children. About midnight he seemed somewhat stronger, and conversed a little with Mr. Bright and Mr. Moffat, M.P., and with two friends and neighbors from Midhurst. As the morning of Sunday, the second of April, dawned, it became clear that death had set his seal upon him. He gradually sank, but, thanks to God's goodness, with a cessation of suffering, and in bodily and mental tranquillity; and just as the church bells were concluding their summoning peals to the houses of God throughout the land, the spiritual essence which had for nearly sixty-one years inhabited a human fabric which the Deity had made very eminently a home of the habitation of His gracious Spirit, returned to Him who gave it, and who providentially directed its energies so largely to the advantage of His human creatures.

CHAPTER XIV.

TRIBUTES TO MR. COBDEN'S MEMORY AND MERITS.

FEW who were living, and of sufficiently matured powers of observation at the time, will ever forget the sad and general impression made by the tidings of Mr. Cobden's peaceful release, throughout the whole land, among all classes of its citizens, and in the great countries of Europe and the New World.   Mr. Cobden, with a patriotism as undeniable and unquenchable as ever animated a human breast, had nevertheless been the great apostle of kindliness and conciliation in international relations, and one consequence was, that he was more beloved and popular out of his own land than ever statesman was in the history of the world.   Englishmen — even those who had admired him most warmly while living — were astounded when they came, after his death, to realize the beauty of his character, the magnitude of his services, and the amount of what they had lost by his somewhat early departure.   They were equally startled to find that France, Germany, Italy, and America mourned him as if he had been a son and citizen of their own soils.   A letter from Paris, dated two days after his death, says: "Last night I happened to be at a *soirée* in a fashionable *salon*. The only topic of conversation was the immense loss even this country has sustained by the death of Mr. Cobden, which, by its suddenness, startled the Parisian world, and has created a painful sensation, as well as a deep feeling of regret." A short paragraph in the list of European telegrams in the daily papers a few days after his death showed that he was so mourned on the distant Danube, that Prince Milosch, of Servia, decreed that services in honor of his memory and for the peace of his soul should be held in the cathedral of Belgrade, and the other churches of the Greek communion in his principality. Thus the gentle influences of his life had not only bridged over the abyss of antipathy between nation and nation, but were revealed at his death to have accomplished the nobler feat of obliterating the more deep-seated disagreements of rival faiths.

In the English House of Commons a scene was witnessed on the day succeeding his death, than which never did any transaction of the six centuries of that assembly's existence redound upon it more infinite credit. To comment upon it would be to mar the dignity and honor of the picture. We present it unabridged, and in a relief unaffected by any fringe or framework of our own.

"On the clerk at the table proceeding to read

the orders of the day, the first of which was the motion to go into committee of supply, Lord Palmerston rose, and, amid breathless silence, said: 'Sir, it is impossible for the House to have this motion put and any determination come to upon it without every member recalling to his mind the great loss which this House and the country have sustained by the event which took place yesterday morning. Sir, Mr. Cobden, whose loss we all deplore, stood in a pre-eminent position, both as a member of this House, and as a member of the British nation. I do not mean, in the few words which I have to say upon this subject, to disguise, or to avoid stating, that there were many matters upon which a great number of people differed from Mr. Cobden — I among the rest; but those who differed from him could never have had any doubt of the honesty of his purpose or the sincerity of his convictions. They felt that his object was the good of his country, however they might differ on particular occasions from him as to the means by which that end was to be accomplished. But we will all leave in oblivion points of difference, and think only of the great and important services he rendered to his country. Sir, it is many years ago since Adam Smith elaborately and conclusively, as far as argument could go, advocated as the fundamental principle of the wealth of nations the freedom of industry and the unrestricted exchange of the objects and results of industry. These doctrines were inculcated by learned men — by Dugald Stewart and others, and were taken up in process of time by leading statesmen, such as Huskisson and those who agreed with him. But the barriers which long-associated prejudice — honest and conscientious prejudice — had raised against the practical application of these doctrines for a great number of years, prevented their coming into use as instruments of progress to the country. To Mr. Cobden it was reserved, by his untiring industry, his indefatigable personal activity, the indomitable energy of his mind, and I may say by that forcible Demosthenic eloquence with which he treated all subjects he took in hand—it was reserved for him, aided, no doubt, by a great phalanx of worthy associates, such as my right honorable friend the President of the Poor-law Board, and by Sir Robert Peel, whose name will be ever associated with the principles he so ably advocated—I say it was reserved for Mr. Cobden, by exertions which were never surpassed, to carry into practical application those abstract principles with the truth of which he was so deeply impressed, and which at last gained the acceptance of all reasonable men in the country. He conferred an inestimable and enduring benefit by the result of those exertions. But, great as were Mr. Cobden's talents, great as was his industry, and eminent as was his success, his disinterestedness

of mind equaled them all. He was a man of
great ambition; his ambition was to be useful to
his country, and that ambition was amply gratified. When this present government was formed
I was authorized graciously by her majesty to offer Mr. Cobden a seat in the cabinet. Mr. Cobden declined, and in doing so he frankly told me
that he thought he and I differed greatly upon
many important questions of political action, and
he therefore thought it would not be comforta-
ble, either to himself or myself, to join the administration of which I was the head. I think
he was wrong; but I will say that no man, however strongly he may have differed from Mr.
Cobden upon general political principles, or the
application of those principles, could have come
into communication with him without carrying
away the strongest personal esteem and regard
for the man with whom he differed. The two
great achievements of Mr. Cobden were — in the
first place, the abrogation of those laws which
limited the importation of corn, which gave a
great development to the industry of the country;
and then the commercial arrangement which he
negotiated with France, and which has also greatly benefited the commercial relations of this country. When the latter achievement was accomplished I knew he would not accept office, and
therefore it was my lot to offer to Mr. Cobden
those honors which the crown can bestow in the

form of a baronetcy and a seat in the Privy Council. These are honorable distinctions which it would have been a gratifying reward to the crown to have bestowed upon him, and I do not think that it would have been at all derogatory for him to have accepted them; but that same disinterested spirit which marked all his conduct, whether public or private, led him to decline these honors, which would have been readily bestowed. I can only say that the country has sustained a loss which all the country must feel. We have lost a man who may be considered to be peculiarly emblematical of the constitution under which all have the happiness to live, because he rose to great eminence in this House, and rose to acquire an ascendency in the public mind, not by virtue of any family connections, but solely and entirely in consequence of the power and vigor of his mind — that power and vigor being applied to purposes evidently advantageous to his country. Sir, Mr. Cobden's name will be forever associated with and engraved on the most interesting pages of the history of this country, and I am sure that there is not a man in this House who does not feel this day the deepest regret that the House has lost one of its brightest ornaments, and the country one of her most useful servants.'

"Mr. Disraeli, whose rising was the signal for cheers from all parts of the House, said: 'Sir, having been a member of this House when Mr.

Cobden first took his seat in it, and having indeed remained in this House during the whole time of his somewhat lengthened Parliamentary career, I can not reconcile myself to silence on this occasion, when we have to deplore the loss of one so eminent, and one, too, in the full ripeness of his manhood and the full vigor of his intellect. Although it was the fortune of Mr. Cobden to enter public life at a time when passions were roused, still, when the strife was over, there was soon observed in him a moderation and temperateness of expression that intimated a large intellectual capacity and high statesmanlike qualities. There was in his character a peculiar vein of reverence for tradition, which often, unconsciously to himself, subdued and softened the severity of the conclusions to which he may have arrived. That, sir, in my mind, is a quality which in some degree must be possessed by any man who attempts or aspires to sway this assembly. Notwithstanding the rapid changes in which we live and the improvements which we anticipate, this country is still Old England. What the qualities of Mr. Cobden were in this House, all now present are able to judge. I think I may say that, as a debater, he had few equals; as a logician, he was close and compact, and I would say adroit, acute, and perhaps even subtle; yet, at the same time, he was gifted with that degree of imagination that he never lost sight of the sympathies of those whom he addressed ; and so, generally avoiding to drive his arguments to an extremity, he became, as a speaker, both practical and persuasive. The noble lord, who is far more competent than myself to deal with such a subject, has referred to his career as an administrator. It seemed to be destined, notwithstanding the eminent position which he had achieved and occupied, and the various opportunities which offered for the ambition which he might legitimately possess, that his life should pass without the opportunity of showing that he possessed those talents and qualities so valuable in the council and in the management of public affairs. But still it fortunately happened that before he quitted us he had one of the greatest opportunities which a public man could enjoy, and in the transactions of great affairs obtained the consideration of the two leading countries of the world. There is something mournful in the history of this Parliament when we remember how many of our most eminent and valuable public men have been removed from among us. I can not refer to the history of any Parliament that will bear down to posterity so fatal a record. But, sir, there is this consolation remaining to us, when we remember our unequaled and irreparable losses, that those great men are not altogether lost to us, that their words will be often quoted in this House, that their examples will often be referred to and appealed to, and that even their expressions may form a part of our discussions. There are, indeed, I may say, some members of Parliament who, though they may not be present, are still members of this House, are independent of dissolutions, of the caprices of constituencies, and even of the course of time. I think that Mr. Cobden was one of those men. I believe that when the verdict of posterity shall be recorded upon his life and conduct, it will be said of him that, looking to his expressions and his deeds, he was without doubt the greatest political character that the pure middle class of this country has as yet produced ; that he was an ornament to the House of Commons, and an honor to England.'

"After a brief and impressive pause, Mr. Bright rose, and, in a voice tremulous with emotion, said : 'Sir, I feel that I can not address the House on this occasion ; but every expression of sympathy which I have witnessed has been most grateful to my heart.' (The honorable gentleman betrayed strong emotion, but recovered himself and proceeded.) 'But the time which has elapsed since I was present when the manliest and gentlest spirit that ever quitted or tenanted a human form departed this life is so short that I dare not even attempt to give utterance to the feelings by which I am oppressed.' (The honorable gentleman here for a moment paused, and covered his face with his hand.) 'I shall leave to some calmer moment,

when I may have an opportunity of speaking before some portion of my countrymen, the exposition of the lesson which I think may be learned
from the life and character of my friend. I have
only to say that after twenty years of most intimate and almost brotherly friendship with him, I
little knew how much I loved him until I found
that I had lost him. (The honorable gentleman,
whose broken words of sorrow were with difficulty spoken, sat down, amid the sympathetic applause of the House.)"

At the monthly dinner of the Société D'Eco-
nomie Politique, in Paris, three days after his
death, Mr. Cobden's memory was honored in the
warmest terms by such men as Hippolyte Passy,
Chevalier, Arles Dufour, and Joseph Garnier.
"Cobden has done more," said the president, M.
Passy, "for allaying international hatreds, for the
extinction of those jealous rivalries which have
so often armed peoples against each other, and for
promoting the fundamental interests of humanity,
than any of the statesmen who have hitherto
taken part in the government of nations. Cobden
is no more, but his works remain, and the future
will honor them, for their wisdom and benefi-
cence will from day to day more distinctly appear."

The foreign minister of France, M. Drouyn de
Lhuys, introducing an admirable innovation in
diplomatic intercourse, sent a dispatch on the all-

engrossing theme to the French embassador in
London, which rivaled in the excellence of its
terms the observations of Mr. Disraeli; and higher eulogy than this could not be accorded to it.
Although in most instances one can do no more
than cull a single leaf from the wreaths of *im-
mortelles* reverently placed on Cobden's tomb,
the importance of this document justifies our
presentation of it unmutilated and sacred from
curtailment:

"To his Excellency the Prince de la Tour d'Auvergne,
   Embassador of France at London, Paris, April 8.

"PRINCE,—A few days since, while the first
minister of her Britannic majesty bore brilliant
testimony in the House of Commons to the memory of Richard Cobden, a speaker belonging to
the government of the Emperor expressed the re-
grets which the death of this illustrious man gave
rise to in France, and the Legislative body identified themselves with this homage by a unanimous impulse.

"A manifestation so honorable to the two nations, and to the person whose loss England de-
plores, will not have escaped your attention, and
you will perhaps have already had occasion to
communicate thereupon with the ministers of the
queen. I desire, nevertheless, prince, to place you
in a position to express to them officially the
mournful sympathy and truly national regret

which the death, as lamented as premature, of Richard Cobden has excited on this side of the Channel.

"That indefatigable promoter of liberty in the domain of commerce and manufactures was not only the living proof of what merit, perseverance, and labor can accomplish, but one of the most complete examples of those men who, sprung from the most humble ranks of society, raise themselves to the highest ranks in public estimation by the effect of their own worth and of their personal services ; finally, one of the rarest examples of the solid qualities inherent in the English character. He is, above all, in our eyes, the representative of these sentiments and those cosmopolite principles before which national frontiers and rivalries disappear; while essentially of his country, he was still more of his time; he knew what mutual relations could accomplish in our day for the prosperity of peoples. Cobden, if I may be permitted so to say, was an international man.

"There are some mental views and aptitudes which are only given to those who in the outset of their career have felt the embarrassments and the difficulties of life, who have had to struggle against the necessities of a position less than humble. Richard Cobden had been brought up in this severe but strengthening school; he thence derived, as the best preparation for a knowledge of political economy, the gift of sympathy with the sufferings of the laborious classes in the midst of whom he had lived; he understood the better the straitened circumstances which he had shared; and in feeling the need of alleviating them, he was naturally led to seek the means to do so — firstly, in the abolition of the Corn Laws in England, then in the suppression or lowering of the barriers which the various commercial laws had raised between peoples. Certainly Cobden did not create any of the principles of industrial and commercial liberty. They had been professed and propagated before him by eminent theorists in England and France. But his glory is to have followed up the practical application of them, abroad and at home, with an ardor and devotedness quite unparalleled.

"Exempt from national prejudices as from those of education and caste, Richard Cobden brought to the pursuit of reforms which he judged useful to his country and profitable to humanity a disinterestedness and a sincerity which one can not but honor, while at the same time one is obliged to admit that all his views were not equally practicable.

"For ourselves, we can not forget the considerable part he took in the change of opinions which prepared, and in the negotiations which led to, the treaty of commerce at present existing between France and England. This important act, the good results of which experience has already consecrated, and the liberal provisions of which are from day to day adopted by other powers of Europe, will have for effect not only the development of the material interests between England and France, but it will also aid powerfully in strengthening their friendly relations. This was the double object of Richard Cobden. He loved and understood France better than any other person, and regarded as one of the greatest interests of his country and humanity the maintenance of peaceful relations between the two nations, which, according to the expression recently used by a member of the English cabinet, march at the head of the world.

"You will be good enough, prince, to acquaint the first minister and the principal secretary of her Britannic majesty with the sentiments expressed in this dispatch, and which they will receive, I doubt not, with a willingness equal to that which has dictated them. Receive, etc.,

"(Signed), DROUYN DE LHUYS."

After a long and elaborate sketch of his life, the writer of an admirable article in the *Moniteur* thus concluded:

"A special and peculiarly admirable characteristic of the man whom England has just lost renders the loss one which must be felt alike by Europe and by the whole world. He was the type of the true economist, the citizen of the commercial universe. Most sincerely attached to British interests, he did not separate them from those of other peoples. He saw the development and the greatness of his own country in the development and the greatness of rival nations, for he understood no rivalries but those of peace. Thus he passed a part of his life in traveling from country to country, preaching his industrial crusade, spreading his doctrines, employing every where his favorite weapon—persuasion, ... Cobden was able to understand France, and he loved her —she will never forget him."

In the Corps Legislatif the subject of Cobden's death was introduced by its vice-president, M. Forcade la Roquette, and his warm expressions of esteem were applauded and repeated on every hand. "The death of Richard Cobden," he said —"and I feel convinced that the Chamber will cordially join in the sentiment—is not alone a misfortune for England, but a cause of mourning for France and for humanity." The Emperor took means of letting his personal sympathy with the expressions of his subjects appear by declaring his intention to place a bust of the great Free Trader in his palace of Versailles.

From Germany there were similar tributes— from the Prussian Chambers and in the pages of the great newspapers. The *Cologne Gazette* con-

cluded a lengthened biography in these words:
"How high stands such a man, in whom the
rising citizenhood, the enlightened spirit of our
age, were, so to speak, incorporated! How, in
comparison with him, do all the petty vanities
and ridiculous pretensions of caste conceit sink
into pitiful nonentity!"

At the conclusion of a lecture delivered before
the Leeds Mechanics' Institution two days after
Cobden's death, Elihu Burritt, speaking in behalf
of America, said:

"When such a man lies dead in the land;
while the shadow of a great sorrow is on a nation's face, and millions in other countries feel the
penumbra of the same grief moving over their
spirits; while the electric wires of the world are
yet thrilling with the news that one of the very
foremost workers in the world's history for the
well-being of mankind has just gone to his rest, I
could not refrain on this occasion from offering a
small tribute of reverence to a memory which, I
trust and believe, the English-speaking race in
both hemispheres will ever hold and cherish as a
common treasure. If, in the grand words of the
ablest of his political opponents, such a man, in
the working presence of his great mind, is still a
member of Parliament, ' independent of dissolutions, of the caprice of constituencies, and even
of the course of time,' he is in a wider sweep of
influence an immortal citizen of the great com-

monwealth of states that speak the earth-engir-
dling tongue whose latent power his peerless logic
unlocked and strengthened to its utmost capacity
of expression in the advocacy of principles that
shall live forever among men—among the brightest immortalities of truth and right. All the
millions that inhabit the American continent shall
hold the life of Richard Cobden as one of the
great gifts of God to a common race, and cherish
and revere his memory as one of the priceless
heir-looms which the motherland has presented
to the multitudinous family of states she has
planted on the outlying continents and islands
of the globe. In the proud and grateful sentiment of this relationship, they shall say *we* share
with her in the common patrimony of such a life,
and feel they have a children's right to light the
lamp of their experience by its light, and follow
its guidance, without abstracting from the beams
it sheds around her feet."

At home, in England, the corporations of London and the provincial towns, as well as the
Chambers of Commerce, the associations of working men, and other bodies, hastened to pass resolutions of regretful respect and of condolence with
Mr. Cobden's family. One address of condolence
to Mrs. Cobden from a provincial Reform Club—
that of Blackburn—was distinguished by the deli-
cate kindliness and sympathy of its tone. " We
did not," it stated, " love your husband at a dis-

tance; his nature was too kindly and tender; all were drawn toward him." One who has a just right to speak on behalf of the more intelligent members of the industrial order thus truthfully expressed himself:

" He was one of the few members of Parliament who thought for the people, and, what is more and rarer, gave himself trouble to promote their interests. He never knew apathy or selfishness. To a clear intellect he united perfect sincerity and a quick conscience. On the question of Reform he kept clear of all that base, paltering, and treacherous indifference which so many others have displayed. He never explained away a promise: he always kept faith with the workman as well as with the gentleman. He cared for principle, not to serve his own ends, but the ends of the people. With him a great principle was a living power of progress; and not to apply it, and produce by it the good which was in it, seemed to him a crime. To him apathy was sin. A cause might be despised, obscure, or poor: he not only helped it all the same—he helped it all the more. He aided it openly and intentionally. Fresh from the honors of great nations, who were proud to receive him as a guest, he would give an audience to a deputation of poor men. The day after he arrived from the court of an emperor, he might be found wending his solitary way to a remote street to attend a committee meeting, to give his personal advice to the advancement of some forlorn hope of progress. In the day of triumph he shrank modestly on one side, and stood in the common ranks; but in the dark or stormy days of unfriended truth he was always to the front."

The Bishop of Oxford, who was prevented by illness from being present at the last rites of his friend and fellow-philanthropist, wrote a most touching letter of regret for his inability to attend the funeral, in which he said, "I feel his loss deeply. I think it is a great national loss. But my feelings dwell rather on the loss of such a man, whom I hope it is not too much for me to venture to call my friend. His gentleness of nature; the tenderness and frankness of his affections; his exceeding modesty; his master love of truth; and his ready and kindly sympathy— these invested him with an unusual charm for me. How deeply I feel for his wife and for his daughters!"

The universal press, of all the shades of politics, added its unanimous tribute. And it was noticed that a large proportion of the biographies and comments which appeared in the newspapers evinced in their writers considerable personal and familiar knowledge of the man. It was remembered that the Corn Law agitation had been a great educational movement as well as one of physical amelioration, and that it had raised many meritorious men from the humbler ranks into its employ as the lecturers of the League, many of whom, at its dissolution, entered upon the honorable career of journalism. These men looked upon Cobden as their great master, and were enabled to communicate to those to whom they discharged the duty of political and economic instruction many personal traits and incidents of Cobden's public life, especially in its earlier and more energetic era.

The *Times* said, "His eminence in the state is, and must always remain, indisputable. The Liberal ranks are too often filled with men whose only claim to distinction is their ability to repeat the catchwords of a party. Mr. Cobden had nothing in common with those echoes." "Richard Cobden," said the *Daily News*, "was more than a Cæsar. When he had done all this, he accepted simply the offering which the nation made him in lieu of the fortune he had sacrificed, and without even the false modesty of a pompous retirement, he continued to render such services as an ordinary member of Parliament can perform. . . . . . . Perfect probity, absolute sincerity, an eager, almost an impetuous desire to make truth triumphant, a belief in the power of human honesty and good feeling, if it could only have fair scope, an incapacity to recognize that rank or privilege conferred dignity or desert—these were the conspicuous virtues or the faults of his character." One sentence in the obituary notice of

the *Manchester Examiner* is as much characterized by its truth as it is by its pith — "He loved
his country not less than any man living, but he
loved it in wise and philanthropic subordination
to the welfare of all mankind." A writer in the
Scotsman, with the accustomed exercise of that
nice critical faculty which has ever distinguished
the great Whig organ of the North, justly pointed
out the fact that "by natural temperament and
tastes Mr. Cobden was by no means an agitator,
much less a demagogue. He was naturally quiet,
unassuming, even timid, and full of a gentleness of
spirit which shone out in his manner, and which
must have made controversy distasteful. He was
cradled into oratory by wrong—a sense of injustice drew him from his parlor to the platform,
and sustained him through a dreary, protracted,
and wearying struggle." Mr. Miall, Mr. Cobden's
friend and fellow-combatant in many fights for
all kinds of freedom — religious, political, and fiscal — thus testified in the *Nonconformist* : "To
do the good he was qualified to do was the only
reward he ever craved. Wealth, ease, reputation,
popularity, social distinction, were all as nothing
when he had a duty to do. When that duty had
been done, he was satisfied. He cared not to
claim the merit. He delighted in lavishing it
upon those with whom he had been associated.
You might be in his company for days together
without hearing a single expression calculated to

remind you of his own superiority of position. He seemed to have no self-consciousness save for what he took to be his defects. He assumed no airs of authority. He recoiled from the very appearance of acting the great man. His affections all tended outward. He was the soul of generosity. But in one respect he firmly and tenaciously held his own — he never parted with his convictions—he would suffer no blandishments to rob him of his self-respect. There were times when he was beset by temptations that would have been powerful for other men. None of them moved him. He put them aside and went on his way, neither caring to deny nor glorying in what he had done."

Time was when, upon the death of such a man, the whole air would have been filled with elegiac odes. We of these days are, for the most part, content with prose. Nevertheless, poetry has not died out of us. We listen with responsive enthusiasm to the truly inspired singer. It is because we believe the following verses equally worthy of the subject and the poet—Cobden and Eliza Cook—that we select them to bind up the garland which we have culled:

> "Cobden! proud, English, yeoman name!
>   I offer unto thee
>   The earnest meed that all should claim
>   Who toil 'mid Slander, Doubt, and Blame,
>   To make the free more free.

"Thy voice has been among the few
  That plead for Human Right;
It asked for justice; and it grew
Still louder when the fair and true
  Were trampled down by Might.

"Thy heart was warm, thy brain was clear,
  Thy wisdom prompt in thought;
Thy manly spirit knew not fear,
But held its country's good most dear—
  Unwarped, unbribed, unbought.

"An open foe—a changeless friend—
  Thy gauntlet pen was flung;
More ready in thy zeal to lend
A shield to others, than defend
  Thyself from traitor's tongue.

"A home-bred Cæsar thou hast been,
  Whose bold and bright career
Leaves on thy brow the wreath of green,
On which no crimson drop is seen,
  No widow's bitter tear."

CHAPTER XV.

THE GRAVE.

Our task is now all but complete. It only remains to reproduce the circumstances of the transit of the earthly remains of Richard Cobden to that God's-acre which he himself had indicated as his chosen resting-place, and where the father and the son now lie side by side. We would not willingly withhold from our readers the advantage of having the picture of the funeral presented in the very words of a witness of, and participant in, the sad ceremony—a privilege which the writer of these pages did not enjoy. We make, therefore, no apology for, and believe, indeed, that we rather enhance the value of our record by presenting the account of Mr. Cobden's burial in the very words of that authority of whom we have already made such large use.

"The mourners, who numbered several hundreds, formed a procession half a mile or more in length. They walked at a funeral pace along the picturesque highway which leads direct to West Lavington Church. At many points on the road groups of country people were gathered, who had put on such mourning as they could command, and whose honest faces expressed the sorrow they felt. The shingled spire and oaken porch of West Lavington Church presently caught the eye, and in a few minutes the base of the hill upon which the church stands was reached, and Religion was about to consecrate with its solemn rites Death's last great achievement. The procession was then re-formed. Passing through the Lychgate, where in olden times the mourners were accustomed to engage in prayer, the coffin was borne by laborers on Mr. Cobden's estate up the steep pathway. The pall was held by twelve of Mr. Cobden's most distinguished associates: Mr. Bright, M.P.; the Right Hon. W. E. Gladstone, M.P.; the Right Hon. Charles Pelham Villiers, M.P.; Mr. George Wilson, formerly chairman of the Anti-Corn-Law League; the Right Hon. Thomas Milner Gibson, M.P.; Mr. Moffatt, M.P.; Mr. Thomas B. Potter, Mr. A. W. Paulton, Mr. Henry Ashworth; Mr. Bazley, M.P.; Mr. William Evans, chairman of the Emancipation Society; and Mr. Thomas Thomasson. The chief mourners then followed: Mr. Charles Cobden, the brother of the deceased; Mr. William Sale, of Manchester, his brother-in-law; Mr. John Williams, the brother of Mrs. Cobden; Mr. Frederick Hogard, Mr. Charles F. Kirk, and Mr. William Sale, jun., relatives of the family; and Mr. Rhoades, Mr. Fisher, sen., and Mr. Fisher, jun. Half way up the ascent the coffin was placed on the bier, and carried up the successive terraces of the grave-yard into the peaceful house of prayer, where it was deposited in the chancel between the choir stalls. As Mr. Bright ascended the church steps he was tenderly supported by Mr. Gladstone, who, by his presence, paid the last tribute of respect to his distinguished friend. The church, which from this day forth is destined to have a memorable historic interest, is built in the middle pointed style, and was erected as recently as 1850, the last act of Archbishop Manning before he seceded to the Roman Catholic Church having been to watch over its completion. If the exterior is attractive, the inside view exhibits a singularly successful combination of taste and simplicity. The roof is supported by a double row of massive arches and columns. The screen is made of Petworth marble, and is tastefully carved. The sculptured brackets and corbels represent the fern and wild hops of the district. The frontal of the altar and the draperies of the pulpit and the lectern are at present of violet cloth, the color of the Lenten season. Above all, the stained glass of the eastern window typifies, by its sublime figures, the great truth of the Resurrection, and is at once the symbol of our Lord's second coming, and of that exalted faith which yesterday must have brought consolation to every heart. The church is only adapted to accommodate two hundred persons, the exact number of souls dwelling in the little parish of Lavingup. On this occasion it was wholly inadequate to receive the large concourse that had assembled. It was soon full to overflowing, and hundreds who failed to procure admission were compelled to take up their position on one or other of the terraces into which the grave-yard, standing, as it does, on the slope of a hill, is necessarily laid out. The opening sentences of the beautiful service for the dead—that immortal legacy which has been bequeathed to us by the piety of our forefathers, and which is destined to be transmitted to the latest generations—were read by the Rev. James Currie, M.A., the incumbent of the parish. The lesson from that chapter of the Corinthians in which the great apostle proclaims the grand doctrine of the resurrection of the body in language as majestic as it was truly inspired by the Most High, was read by the Rev. Caleb Collins, M.A., the rector of Stedham and Heyshot, Mr. Cobden's own parish. Then the body, with these heaven-sent words of faith and hope still ringing in the ears of the mourners, was carried out into the bright sunshine, which beamed with celestial splendor upon the scene. No one present could have wished that Mr. Cobden had been buried in any other spot. The magnificence of the abbey or the minster paled before the glory of nature's beauteous temple. From the crest of that hill upon which his remains were so soon to mingle with their mother dust, the eye gazed upon a landscape as charming and resplendent as Milton's picture of Paradise. In the far distance, forming a background on the horizon, stretched the range of the South Downs from Worthing in the east to Petersfield in the west, a distance of thirty miles. Between lay the valley of the hills, thickly wooded with pine, and fir, and oak, the foliage of which reflected every color, and gleamed with the rays of a warm spring sun. There was a quietude and a peace in it all which the busy haunts of men can never give, even when one treads the stately aisles of Westminster or St. Paul's. No wonder that long years ago—before the death of his only and well-beloved son—Mr. Cobden should not only have chosen this church-yard as his future burial-place, but have selected for his grave the very spot where yesterday he was interred; for, wherever the eye wanders from this central point, it rests upon scenes of pastoral loveliness which can not be surpassed in any part of this beautiful isle.

"Mr. Cobden's vault lies at the southern extremity of the grave-yard, and its only occupant until yesterday was his son, who died in Germany, but whose remains were buried here. In allowing a vault to be constructed at all, the incumbent exhibited a graciousness of disposition which, taking into account the strength of his opinions, deserves a cordial recognition. Around the gaping

T

vault clustered the mourners and bosom friends and political associates of Mr. Cobden. There stood his brother and his kindred. There Mr. Gladstone, with eyes closed and face unnaturally pale. There Mr. Bright, whose manly grief was that of a brother. There Mr. George Wilson, Mr. A. W. Paulton, and Mr. William Evans, who had been associated with him in the earlier struggles as well as the later triumphs of the Anti-Corn-Law League. There also stood Mr. Milner Gibson and Mr. Villiers, who, like him, were leaders in the warfare against an unrighteous monopoly. There was a singular fitness in the presence of the three cabinet ministers who are the appointed guardians of the interests of finance, trade, and the impoverished classes, and who come here to render homage to the ashes of the man who was the liberator of commerce and the champion of the poor. Lord Clarence Paget, another representative of the government, was present; so also was Lord Alfred Paget, who represented the court."

Among many other mourners were Mr. Adams, the American minister, Lord Kinnaird, Mr. Bazley, M.P., Mr. J. B. Smith, M.P., Mr. Baines, M.P., Mr. W. E. Forster, M.P., Mr. Moran, the Secretary of the American Legation, Mr. Charles Gilpin, M.P., Mr. Stansfeld, M.P., Mr. Leatham, M.P., Sir Morton Peto, Mr. Edward Miall, Mr. John Richardson, who carried a motion in the Corporation of London that a marble bust of Mr. Cobden should be placed in their Council Chamber, Mr. Robertson Gladstone, the Rev. Newman Hall, Dr. Hook, the Dean of Chichester, Mr. Thomas B. Potter, Mr. Cobden's successor in the representation of Rochdale, the Rev. Henry Richard, M. Visschers, the eminent Belgian statesman, the Rev. Dr. Brock, Mr. Elihu Burritt, Mr. Samuel Morley, and a host of other well-known men.

Loving hands had woven chaplets of everlasting and new spring flowers, which were deposited with reverent care on the foot of the coffin; and one venerable individual, who had come a long journey, being unable to approach the grave, handed the flowers which he had gathered from one to another, that they might be placed by the side of the other mementoes of affection. Slowly the coffin was pushed down the narrow planks as the priest solemnly pronounced the words, "Earth to earth, ashes to ashes, dust to dust," and cast upon the lid a handful of that clay which is the emblem of mortality. As the coffin passed from view, Mr. Bright, with irrepressible grief, advanced nearer and nearer, and strained his eyes into the narrow tomb which was so soon to be closed. The sorrow of many found vent in audible sobs; but the comforting benediction closed the painful scene, and the grief-stricken throng separated after taking another and yet another farewell of the resting-place of the great and good

Richard Cobden. He sleeps the long sleep on the lovely summit of a Sussex hill—not in a wilderness of graves, for there are few who share that consecrated ground with him, but amid scenes which speak of the beauty of his life and the glorious hope of a joyful resurrection.

The author of an article in "All the Year Round," describing "Richard Cobden's Grave," thus wrote:

"There was a deep sadness in every face, tears in women's eyes, and the bell from the lofty belfry tolled with a plaintive tinkle. About two hundred gentlemen filled the little church, in which service was read, with mumbling mutterings. When the coffin was borne out of the church, and along the terrace toward the grave, amid the uncovered mourners, the sun beating warmly upon their heads, while the clergyman said "dust to dust," "in hope," and the coffin grated down the planks into the vault, a shock of grief passed through the crowd of mourners, women wept, and men grew deadly pale. Many of the hands there had often been warmly clasped during a severe political struggle by the hand lying there dead. A French wreath of everlastings was laid on the coffin above his feet, and a wreath of spring flowers—blue and purple anemones, primroses, polyanthuses, hepaticas, primulas, above his breast. It was an aged man of fourscore years who handed forward the wreath of spring flow-

ers, and who had commenced his friendship with
the deceased on the Catskill Mountains, in America, in July, 1835. This old man's chaplet was
but the first of many symbols of respect paid to
the memory of a man whose name is significant
of a commercial policy tending to give the poor
their daily bread, and spread peace on earth and
good-will among men."

A friend remarked to us a few days after the
death of Cobden that the three great attitudes
and performances of his life were valuable in the
inverse ratio of their popularity — that his Anti-
Corn-Law agitation, which bulked most largely
in connection with his name in the public eye,
was really a less wondrous feat, and less productive of great future consequences, than the French
Treaty ; for the latter was a recognition and declaration of the principle of the extension to the
whole world of the advantages confined by the
former to England. And similarly, that Cobden's unswerving advocacy of universal peace
and arbitration betwixt differing and alienated
nations was really something larger and grander
than his purely fiscal achievements. We agreed
perfectly with the remark. After all, the most
splendid legacy left by Cobden was his preaching
of " Peace on Earth." At a Peace Society Meeting at Newcastle shortly after Cobden's death,
his friend, the Rev. Henry Richard, the excellent
and estimable Secretary of the Peace Society,

feelingly and forcibly impressed this fact. And we believe that we can not more fitly conclude our narrative of the life of this God-sent man— for we believe we could not do so in a manner more likely to be approved by Mr. Cobden's own gentle spirit—than by the citation of these heart-felt, earnest, and memorable words:

"Last Friday I stood over the grave of Richard Cobden, and, to confess my weakness, when I looked into the vault and saw his coffin lie there, and recall to remembrance how long that man had been like a tower of strength to me upon which I could always lean—his wisdom in council and his undaunted courage in action—the first impulse of my weakness was as if I must retire from all share in public matters, and give them up in despair and despondency. A few months before, I had walked by his side along the same road where the funeral procession went on Friday, and I could remember the precise remarks he made to me by the particular points of the road, and my feeling was, as I said, having lost such a pillar of strength in the cause of peace, that I could no longer persevere; but my second reflection was, that such is not the lesson which the life and example of Richard Cobden should attach to any of his surviving friends—that man who, twenty-five years ago, lifted up his voice in the midst of this nation in favor of Free Trade and international peace, and who continued, till the last day of his life, faithful and unflinching to the principles of his youth.   Was it right, then, that I should retire from the work which Providence has given to me to do?   No, I would rather be as the Carthaginian general, taking a little boy to his father's bosom to swear true enmity to Rome.   So I felt disposed, standing over the grave of my honored and beloved friend, whose friendship had been for fifteen years the privilege and pride of my existence, that I would rather swear true fidelity to the cause of peace, a cause for which he had done more than any man of his age; and I would, if it had been in my power, have taken hundreds of the rising youth of England, and there, over the grave of the man of peace, have sworn them all to an unflinching fidelity to the same cause."

INDEX.

Newspaper press, eulogium by Cobden on, 227; tributes by, to his memory, 280.

Nicholas, Czar of Russia, Cobden's opinion of, 175, 181, 191.

Oastler, Richard, his career and public services, 46, 141.

O'Connell, Daniel, great Free Trade speech at Manchester, 52.

O'Connor, Feargus, his opposition to the League, 44; character of, 141; rebuked by Cobden, 159.

Otway, birthplace of, 15.

Overstone, Lord, unsuccessfully contests Manchester, 27; joins the League, 121.

Oxford, Cobden's opinion on education at, 244.

Oxford, Bishop of, tribute to Cobden's memory, 280.

Palmerston, Lord, his foreign policy first attacked by Cobden, 31; blamed by Cobden for his conduct to the Hungarians, 181; attack by him on Cobden, 201; his government defeated by Cobden on the China War, 210; appeals successfully to the country, 213; offers Cobden a seat in the cabinet, 215; and public honors, 223; his tribute to Cobden's memory, 264.

Paper duty. See Taxes on Knowledge.

Parliamentary Reform, opinions of Cobden on, 159, 164, 244.

Pattison, Mr., returned as first Free Trade member for City of London, 121.

Paulton, A. W., first enlistment in the Anti-Corn-Law cause, 39; engaged as the first lecturer of the League, 40; his services, etc., 51.

Peace Society, Cobden's services to, 168–184; real character of, 169.

Peel, Sir Robert, leading incidents of his administration, 68, 73; budget of 1842, 82; parliamentary encounters with Cobden, 89, 90, 93, 111, 128; eulogiums on Cobden, 113, 114, 137; abolition of Corn Laws, 133.

Peterloo Massacre, Free Trade Hall built on scene of, 52.

Phillips, Mark, first Free Trade member for Manchester, 26, 66.

Place, Francis, an early Free Trader, 36.

Potter, T. B., M.P., letter of Cobden to, 255, 256.

Prentice, Archibald, makes Cobden's acquaintance, 22; describes Cobden's first enlistment in the Free Trade ranks, 29; a member of the first London Association, 36; his

THE END.